PRAISE FOR *THE BLOOD ZODIAC* SERIES

"Erica Crockett burst onto the literary scene in 2014 with her debut psychological suspense novel, *Chemicals*. Now she is quick to follow up with an episodic serial tour de force worthy of *True Crime*, proving she is also on her way to establishing herself as a master of the thriller genre. It's hard to believe that such an accomplished talent is only just getting started."

- Vincent Zandri, New York Times and USA Today Bestselling author of *The Remains* and *Everything Burns*

"*The Ram* is one of those books that will have you skipping meals to find out what happens next. It's an expertly plotted and addictive character-driven work of art. Take notice, people. Erica Crockett has arrived!"

- David M. Brown, Editor-In-Chief, 5th Dimension Comics

"Riley and Peach are running the show. Our experience is in their hands, and their desires, insecurities, short-comings, and violent lust. With time we realize a larger force is at work, thrusting Riley and Peach against one another. I have the sense that Ms. Crockett is being used in the same way to channel a myth much bigger than herself. The story is telling itself through her, propelling her words deliberately towards a destined and inevitable outcome."

- Jon Keithley, Author of *Shivertown*

THE RAM

CYCLE 1 OF
THE BLOOD ZODIAC

ERICA CROCKETT

Corvid Tear Media

Printed in the United States of America

ISBN 978-1-942300-03-8

First Printing, 2016

Cover Design by Jenny Flint

Published by Corvid Tear Media
Boise, Idaho
www.corvidtearmedia.com

FOR THOSE BORN UNDER THE SIGN OF ARIES

Erin Crockett

All the good children let visionary leaders select suitable characteristics, assign personalities.

-    Peach Barrow

MONDAY, THE 23RD OF MARCH, 2015

MONDAY, THE 23RD OF MARCH, 2015

01   RILEY

All the fight has left him.

Riley believed before, when life seemed to always take his side no matter his dubious choices and rough spells, that he'd be a solid contender for making it from birth to death with minimal tears in his body and his spirit. But a few years ago, life soured on him, and he couldn't get his sweetheart back. No matter how he wooed her. That former paramour, she was a fickle bitch. Just like most mortal women. Except life was the only lover with longevity, staying power, the only one he'd been in a relationship with all these years. But now, Riley felt as though life was keen on seeing him buried and gone at an early age.

"Go ahead and check the chains again," Double Al shouts at Riley. His boss reminds him of a bear standing on hind legs, thick with rings of both muscle and fat. The man's notable features are the tight white and black curls cut close to his scalp and lips the size of Riley's thumbs held tightly together. He has a fondness for candy and for Riley, whom he's known for decades, and this is how Riley finds himself running his fingers around the cool iron of an anvil. Double Al, the man whose nickname was derived from a word play on his girth and double-wide trailers, nods to the London Anvil cradled in a cross of linking metal chains and then lays a hand on the anvil horn. The unyielding tine is several shades darker than the skin of Double Al, the owner of High Desert Trommel.

"Check this," Riley says under his breath and grabs his crotch. He does it not because he means insult, but because he wants to show his boss his own thoughts on manhood and that he, too, can play the game.

His boss hears the quip and smirks. "Don't have my reading glasses around my neck, son. Afraid I can't get close enough to see it."

Those others who catch the exchange laugh, their hands busy hammering out sides of trommel cylinders or plunging red, runny metal into dark, cold water. Riley is accustomed to being mocked in front of his coworkers. They are men who did not have a track scholarship to Stanford or know the difference between a pleat and pin tuck. He goes along with it now, the crotch grab a new habit, realizing after a few rough weeks at the beginning of his job, that if he put up a fight, they'd only kick him down harder. He couldn't stand apart from them. Riley learned he'd have to meld, to blend. In order for the shop to run smoothly, they'd need to be steel; Riley decided to be the carbon mixed to their iron. He'd be the element of all life.

Riley stoops to feel the links around the two hundred pound anvil. He doesn't blame his coworkers for ribbing him. He rarely did chores as a child and the only physically taxing job he'd had was when he was a teenager working on a landscaping crew. At his current age of thirty-one, heavy breathing only happened during jogging and sex. To go from practicing contract law to working in a metal fabrication shop rolling out trommels used in gold mining was a bizarre transformation his blue-collar

3

coworkers would not let Riley forget.

He was not one of them, though he wore the same tan work overalls smudged with grease and the heavy-toed work boots. But with what had happened to him recently, life landing a sucker-punch to his solar plexus, he was growing comfortable in his new vocation. He couldn't even pretend his acquiescence to his current state was for show or ambition, that he was actually the proverbial wolf in sheep's clothing. Because Riley felt his teeth were dull and worn, his hide a mess of mange and the sheep, in numbers, could easily trample him to death.

"They're all solid," he shouts from where he crouches. Someone has turned on a circular saw and the warm air of the machine shop becomes fragrant with the shavings of pine. He's run his hands over most of the links, unable to get his fingers around the chain underneath the anvil. He assumes it'll hold. It always has.

"Take it up," he hollers.

Newt Parnwell, partial to NASCAR, gun shows and ballroom dancing competitions, heaves on a chain running up and over a pulley suspended from the ceiling and down to the chains wrapped around the anvil. The anvil with its black horn lifts up on one side and Riley thinks of a rhinoceros at full gallop before noticing the chains aren't balancing the anvil's weight. He needs to reorient the fetters so the metal lifts off the floor in one fluid motion.

"Hold up," he says and shoots his hand up in the air. But someone else has turned on the hood vent at the other end of the workshop, the circular saw still sings, and Newt continues to heave the anvil upward, tugging on sections of chain with fists wrapped in kidskin gloves.

Riley swears to himself, pops up off the floor and waves both arms at the man with the bulging eyes of an ill-bred Shih Tzu. But now the man is focused on watching the pulley overhead as it squeaks with the rubbing of metal against metal.

The anvil, bigger than Riley's chest, is hauled up to his eye level and it pitches dangerously to its left side.

"Hey, you stupid son of a bitch," he yells at the man, whom finally looks at Riley. He shrugs his shoulders and Riley motions for him to stop pulling the piece of metal any higher.

He doesn't hear the snapping sound, not with the clanging of mallets, the fan, the hum of the circular saw drowning out the slightest sound of metal warping under too much pressure. Riley doesn't get a chance to move before he sees the anvil slide neatly from its hammock of chains.

It comes to rest on its face, where bits of metal have been beaten flat time and again. He looks to the anvil, trying to reason how the pitch of the thing could see it end up upside down. He uses his analytical mind to distract himself from the sensation of pain. Because Riley's left foot is underneath the slab of iron, the front of his boot hidden from sight by the mass of metal.

That thought he had weeks ago, about being the carbon to their iron to create steel, now he feels it. Carbon may be the stuff of living beings, but iron is wickedly dense, stolid and without life. It is not subject to the mistress of life. So it is prone to winning. The pain in his foot opens up, like the crack of pinecones to the warmth of late spring and he sucks in air through his nose to snatch up the smell of pine, to keep himself from crying out.

Riley lies back on the concrete floor and watches the chains sway overhead, a solitary link bent and open, jangling and dancing, apart from all the rest.

02   PEACH

It's wet and windy outside, galling attributes of a Boise spring which promises to linger on well into June. Peach hates the cold the most. She dealt with the gray days of January and February but became disheartened when the cream and orange-colored daffodils along her front walk wilted after a day of blooming, petals browned by a biting frost in mid-March. At least the robins trilled in the copses of dogwood and birches around her apartment. They were never solitary, moving in great masses of gray punctuated with flashes of tomato-red from their bellies. They took over her neighborhood, situated on the central bench of Boise, a geological shelf rising up to the south of downtown proper. The harbingers of spring shat on cars and left dried bits of juniper berries on the concrete patio outside her door. Peach had no idea what a giant flock of robins would be called, so when they arrived in droves in late February, she borrowed another moniker and named them a murder of robins.

The absurdity of the name makes her smile now. Why can't

the songbirds so many associate with lengthening days and warmer temperatures have a darker side as well? She imagines their sharp, yellow beaks piercing the flesh of berries with crimson skin and sallow, pulpy innards. A murder of robins.

Peach sits at a small desk in the corner of her living room, the view from her seat looking out over the front of her building. It's a rickety, second-hand piece of furniture made of walnut, mid-century or older, deep gouges crisscrossing its flat surface from the misplaced needle of a mathematician's compass or the delinquent hand of a bored child. The work she's brought home is pushed to the side of the desk and she sends a print job to the laserjet printer perched on the top of a side table to her right. She stands, waits for the paper to clear the feeder and spit back out. It catches on the rollers and she sighs, pulls a little at the corner of the envelope and it comes free, a crease running lengthwise down the center. She stuffs the envelope with its intended contents and uses a small, damp sponge the color of her pale lips to wet the envelope adhesive.

She heads outside barefoot in defiance of the weather, the earth still too cool to feel pleasant on the soles of her feet, and drops the letter in the mail collection box for her apartment. A drip of water off one of the carport gutters splashes against her forehead as she tiptoes past robin crap to get back inside.

Before she reaches her patio, a robin chirrup catches her attention and she sees a lone bird, away from his murderous rabble, riding the air currents as if it were a dipping and pitching cargo ship facing a stormy sea. She watches the creature enjoy the ride, the pleasure of flight, until it alights on a brown length of an ash branch half-torn from the tree in the last major storm. It eyes Peach with black orbs throwing out a silver sheen in the dim light and she wonders if the bird envies her like she envies it.

Peach moves to her next task, heads inside her home and deadbolts the door behind her before walking into her master bathroom. A blue plastic sack from a discount store sits on the counter. She flips on the vanity lights and turns on the red heat-bulb housed in a metal casing in her ceiling. A flow of warmth hits her shoulders and she smiles as she dumps the contents of the bag into the sink.

She picks up a pair of new, sharp scissors with red handles, then an electric razor meant for grooming the necks of men and a plastic disposable razor with a pink handle. She completes her collection by pulling a small cylinder of shaving cream out of the porcelain basin and arranges it all in front of her in order of use: scissors, electric razor, cream that smells of lime, Bic.

Peach removes her t-shirt and jeans, letting them fall into a pile on the faux-tile floor. She stands in front of the bathroom mirror in mismatched underwear, a floral-print, red bra and light pink cotton panties. A solitaire gemstone pendant the size of an eyeball lies against her collarbone. Its oval shape contains swirls of reds, greens and gold.

She gathers her sandy-colored hair from behind her shoulders and lets it fall against her heavy breasts. The length of her hair rests just above her waist, with a strong side part and wispy bangs pushed to the side of her face.

"Gorgeous," she says, running her fingers through it, catching her thumb in a snarl, causing her hair to fluff with static. As a teen, she hated the color of her hair. There was something about being blonde which made her feel obligated to be bubbly and light of heart. She'd threatened to dye it a common, unremarkable medium brown but her mother had forbidden it. But Patti is not here now, with her Pall Mall in one hand and Diet Coke in the other.

Peach fingers a tight fist around the base of her skull, holds onto the hair as if she wrings the neck of a swan, picks up the scissors, and cuts it all off.

The clump of hair cascades to the floor, scattering about her feet like dry grass, harvested wheat. She works over her head with the scissors until the hair is too close to the scalp to shear and she nicks herself with the sharp point of the blades. She blots at the blood with a piece of toilet paper and then takes up the electric razor, plugs it into an outlet behind her toothbrush holder, and flips it on. The buzz, the vibration as it runs over her skull makes her entire body shimmy. The raining of the sharp bits of cut hair onto her shoulders, into her cleavage and down her thighs makes her body feel as though invaded by golden-colored fleas.

She clicks off the razor, smoothes shaving cream over her skull and uses the disposable blade to relieve her skin of its final vestiges of hair. Using a damp washcloth, she wipes the last of the cream off her scalp and splashes water on her face and head while leaning over her sink, not waiting for the water to warm up coming out of the tap. Her skin tingles. Her cheeks flush red like the robins' undersides. Peach grabs her towel and massages her head, noting the divots and ridges she'd never been able to feel before with a full head of hair. If she were familiar with phrenology, she could make guesses as to what each dent or line meant for her life. A round mound over her left ear might mean an aptitude for fulfilling desires. The short trench over her once delicate fontanel could mark her for greatness.

In the mirror she can see her facial features are sharper with a bald pate and she thinks of the Dalai Lama and Black Friars with their tonsured heads, and wonders if they attain spiritual solemnity with each hair they slice from their skin. She touches her nose, her eyebrows caked in bits of fallen hair. She smiles, her teeth seemingly longer and whiter. She brings the stone around her neck up to her lips and presses a kiss on the multi-colored rock.

Digging around in the cupboard under her sink, Peach pulls forth another bag. She sets this on the counter, undoes a double knot constructed with the handles, and pulls out a mass of hair. She sets the wig on her shorn head, tugging at where it hits at the tops of her ears to get it to sit flush against her crown.

Peach takes herself in again, sees that the hair she now wears is nearly identical to the hair she's just lost. The only difference is the shade of blonde. There is a ruddy tint to the wig not present in her natural hair. But she doesn't think most people will notice. Just as most people don't see the breasts of robins aren't a true red, but the muddled tint of pyracantha berries mixed with the pink of nightcrawlers.

"Gorgeous," Peach says as she bends to pick up her clothes, her wig shifting slightly, a plume of spent hair lifting up from the fabric of her t-shirt into the air.

03   RILEY

The pain is all the way to his heart now. At first it resided only in his left foot, a blooming of agony slow at first and then sharp and throbbing. He can't feel his toes; the point nearest to the wound with sensation is the bottom of his ankle. It feels to be pierced with ice shards and poisonous thorns. Riley's eyes are closed but he can hear the men shutting off power tools, their boots scuffing against the floor as they run toward him. The smell of conifer has subsided and now the scent of fresh sweat from his armpits claims its space.

He can hear the booming of Double Al as he shouts, moves aside his employees to get to Riley. Riley knows that his boss is hovering over him. A man with such presence in body and personality has the tendency to loom over those weaker, not to threaten but to aid. Plus, Riley can smell the vinegar of the pickles the man ate at lunch.

"Riley, you with us?" he asks and crouches down to look at the anvil and the foot disappearing beneath it.

Riley opens his eyes and sees the cluster of faces above him. One face belongs to the big-eyed brute responsible for the anvil at rest on Riley's foot. Or maybe only partially responsible. He shuffles up to rest on his forearms and bites his lower lip hard.

"We're gonna need to lift this thing off you. You ready?" Double Al waves over four men and they crouch with their employer. He points at three of them. "You'll be lifting, straight up from his foot." Then he nods at the fourth man. "And you'll be gentle with Riley's foot and pull it out of the way from the under the anvil. You hear me? Nod and verbal affirmation, please."

His coworkers grunt, nod, shake out hands and pop their knuckles. There is no countdown or preparation for the task. Double Al grasps the horn of the anvil as if he could pull the pronged beast off Riley himself and the other three men array themselves around the iron. The boss shouts out, "lift!" and the boys do. The fourth man, hands blackened with soot, cups Riley's foot at the ankle and pulls his leg away from the anvil before it's placed back on the concrete with a dull thud.

The movement of his leg causes bile to rise in Riley's throat, but he chokes it down as he cries out in pain. His coworkers stay silent and don't dare to make light of the situation. Double Al moves to him and hooks one arm under Riley's neck and the other beneath his knees.

"Don't you dare carry me out of here," he whispers to his boss. "I know I'm smaller than you, but I'll never live it down with these assholes."

Double Al frowns but changes position, lifting Riley up at his armpits. Riley puts all his weight on his right foot and the man with the ash-covered hands disappears for a moment and returns with a length of PVC pipe with a T-juncture threaded onto the end. It serves as a decent makeshift crutch and Riley sets his lips into a line but nods at the man in thanks all the same.

The trip out to Double Al's Dodge Ram takes ten minutes at a slow, agonizing pace but Riley refuses the suggestion they call an ambulance. "Do you know how much those things cost?" he says as he limps over pebbles and sand in the dirt parking lot. His boot still hides whatever mess has been made of his foot. He keeps his eyes ahead, focused on moving forward, so he won't be crippled with worry and justifiable anxiety.

Riley only allows himself to be lifted for a moment by Double Al so he can heave himself up into the passenger seat of the vehicle. He bumps his foot on the door and lets out a scream that gets muffled when his boss slams the door and rushes around to the driver's seat. To distract himself from the agony, he tries to remember if Double Al has ever picked him up before and recalls a vague memory of a sprained ankle at a junior high track meet and Riley's father lifting and walking on one side of his body with Double Al on the other, both of his feet floating over the rubber, sepia track.

Double Al steps on the metal foot rail and pulls his large frame into the truck. Riley notices how hard his boss is breathing, taking in short, tight breaths. He's strong, but he's out of shape and nearing retirement. Double Al keys on the ignition and fumbles to turn down the country music that blasts from the dashboard. The singer's nasal voice relates a ballad about hunting dogs and shelled peanuts.

The truck is a 1993, its shocks and struts old, and the trip passes painfully for Riley. He grits his teeth tightly as they speed over potholes and roads under construction. To keep his attention off his foot, Riley stares at a large chunk of iron pyrite hung from the rearview mirror. Fool's gold. It catches the light as it swings left and right in wild arcs.

"You check those chains, Riley?" Double Al asks, his breath settling.

Riley watches the fool's gold, how the sharp angles and lines of the thing shift in color from gold to gray to black depending on how he cocks his head. Anyone who knew anything about gold could see it for what it was. False. Worthless. Good for nothing.

Double Al clear his throat and looks to Riley, tries out a joke. "You must have been playing at being the Road Runner, son." He grins, his double chin lifting with the corners of his mouth.

"I'm not the Road Runner, boss," he says and keeps his eyes on the iron pyrite. The pain tugs at his throat, inches up to the temple on the left side of his head. "It's Wile E. Coyote who always gets the anvil dropped on him."

"Crazy thing is Wile E. Coyote is the one responsible for dropping the anvil on his own stupid head."

Double Al stops his grinning and turns the radio up slightly. A new voice comes through the speakers singing about women, whisky and tumbleweeds.

"You got anyone you want me to call to meet us at the hospital? I can't keep track of your lady friends, Riley. Never could."

The fool's gold keeps up its swinging until Riley reaches up and stops it with his hand. He squeezes it so hard the sharp sides of the rock cut into his flesh and his mind finally swivels to consider the likely state of his foot. He imagines applesauce, homemade, blush pink with bits of Red Delicious skin.

"Hell no," Riley says, "I've got no one for you to call."

04 PEACH

The hairs cleanly removed from her head stick to her fingers
as she sweeps them up with a small broom into a dustpan. Peach
feels elated; a sense of freedom unlike she's experienced since
young childhood takes over her actions. New life seems to come
with bold moves. While she cleans, she's playing, not working,
and the knocking at her front door becomes louder, more
insistent before it breaks her from her revelry and captures her
attention.

She puts down the broom and shuts the bathroom door
behind her. The knocking is harder by the time she gets to the
front door. She wonders if the person on the other side means to
break their hand.

"Peach!" Her name is called out by a voice she knows.

She unbolts the door and Linx pushes it open before she can
officially welcome him inside. He wears a scowl, the lines of his
brow hidden by his choppy, black hair. He's got on a pair of
slim-fit jeans, a tight cardigan and high-top sneakers. He smells

like cilantro.

"I thought you were dead. I didn't hear from you at all last weekend." He shuts the door behind him with his foot and dives for the couch. His Converse shoes hang over the back of the sofa and he sighs heavily.

She eyes him in repose and wonders why such an effeminate and hyperbolic man chooses to be her closest companion. They have little in common when it comes to personality or personal grooming. Peach wiggles her buttocks in near his back and swats his feet down. "You're my best friend, not my handler. I was busy. And you're looking particularly Asian Hipster today."

Linx scrunches up his nose and pokes her in the side. "Did you do something to your hair? It looks a little different. Lowlights?"

"Nope," Peach says, placing both hands on her head to make sure the wig is still there. "Just the same as always."

He sits up and takes Peach's chin in his hands. "Same beauty as always," and plants a kiss on her neck.

He can't see her roll her eyes at the gesture or the way her calves constrict when he plays it off smooth. She knows he wants to be more than best friends with benefits, but she can't give him what he wants. He's kind, funny, and genuine, but he lacks something. Not machismo; she detests the muscle-bound, the aging fraternity brothers. All she knows is she can't even give herself what she wants. At least not yet. So she meets him on middle ground and allows for the sex which means everything to Tuksin "Linx" Lincoln and nothing to her.

She pulls back enough to meet his eyes. They're deep brown, framed by crescent-shaped eyelids. "Let's go to the bedroom. The wicker on this thing gets uncomfortable."

Linx pops up, takes Peach's hands and walks backwards into the bedroom. He whistles the theme song from Jaws as they move toward the bed.

"Are you going to eat me?" Peach asks.

"Maybe," he says, grabbing her about the waist and flinging her onto the bed. "But I've got to use the toilet first."

Linx moves toward the bathroom but Peach stops him with a mild purr before he can open the door and see her blonde hair strewn across the counter, hanging off the bath towels, and matted into the throw rug.

"But I'm ready. Now. Swim back over here, shark boy."

He bounds for the bed, landing on his knees and pulls Peach's legs toward him. He's almost the same weight as Peach, slight and trim due to his Thai mother. He laughs until he notices the new addition to the bed. His fingers run through a lambskin throw in the center of the duvet.

"What the hell is this, Peach? Tell me it's not real."

Peach scoots down so her butt is in the middle of the white wool and works her legs out of her jeans. "It's soft. And I get a sense of what it was like when it was living. The thing has life to it."

"*Had* life to it," Linx corrects her. "Did you forget I'm a vegetarian? Is this some sort of passive aggressive way of telling me you're not into me or that you want me to start cooking you hamburgers? No way are we leaving it on the bed."

"I'll take it off later," she says, "but if you want to have sex, we're having it on the sheepskin. Peach parts her legs slightly and reaches up to pull Linx's shirt and button-down over his head. He shakes out his hair once it's off and Peach casually reaches up to see if her wig is still on straight.

After she says what she wants, he doesn't argue. This trait of Linx's, his willingness to obey, reminds her why she accepts him as a lover and not just her primary confidant. He is the first man she has ever been with who has not demanded to be dominant in the bed and in every facet of partnership. He kisses her body in totality, covering every limb and curve. When he slips inside of her, Peach goes far away. She sees a stage. On it is

17

a woman working a pole, her breasts enormous and fake, her red hair cut in an asymmetrical A-line. Her thighs grip the pole and she cheats gravity with spins around the hard length of chrome. There is music playing but Peach doesn't know the song. A resonating bass drum pervades the song and the stripper works harder, works up a sweat, loses her top, then her tiny shorts.

Peach locks eyes with the woman dancing in her head. The fantasy woman, the stripper, says two words and Peach hugs Linx in tighter to her chest, her body contracting with shudders of pleasure.

"I'm it."

05   RILEY

There are two children with rasping coughs, an elderly woman wheeling around a colostomy bag, and a teenager with a cold pack against his forehead in the emergency room. A nurse stands with her arms crossed as a woman wearing a track suit screams in her face about the pain in her abdomen. She tells the nurse it feels like there are mice inside her guts, gnawing away at pieces of her innards. The nurse repeats over and over again with a monotone voice that drugs are not administered by the nurses in the ER for stomach aches.

Riley is waved into a private intake room of St. Al's Hospital by another nurse with a clipboard held down the front of his thighs. Double Al still acts as a living crutch and the PVC piping helps keep the pressure off his foot. Riley feels a little smug about cutting ahead of all the other people in the waiting room. At least extreme physical trauma gets him pushed to the front of some lines.

"Take a left two doors down and get yourself up onto the

exam table. I'll fetch Doctor Lemic to come in and see what's wrong, okay?"

The nurse walks off and Riley turns his neck toward Double Al. "Yeah, it'll take a really smart doctor to figure out what happened. Gee, doctor," mocks Riley, "I have this bunion on my big toe and it just seems to be acting up more than usual." Riley forces himself to laugh at his own joke, to use a chuckle to distract himself from the agony. The pain radiates out from his foot and affects the rest of his form as if the site of trauma is a distant sun, a dim star, holding sway over all things in his universe, no matter how far away.

Double Al maneuvers himself into the little exam room before Riley, placing a hand on his chest to stop him from trying to walk on his own. He doesn't allow Riley a chance to protest; he lifts him off his feet and places him on the exam table. The motion dishevels his boss's work coveralls. Double Al tugs at the zipper running the length of his torso before swiping a magazine off a spare chair and collapsing into it.

The tissue paper lining on the table crinkles under Riley's slightly padded tan pants. He leaves smudges of dirt and grease on the pristine whiteness. The pain is still unbearable. He looks down to his boot and wonders if he should pull his foot out of it before the doctor gets there, so he can assess the damage on his own. It's only now he notices his foot is surrounded by liquid, cool and thick. Some of his nerve endings are noting wetness instead of pulsing out the same distress signal again and again. He bends over and shoves a finger into the top of his boot and pulls it out. It's covered in blood just beginning to coagulate.

"Keep your hands out of there," Double Al commands as he absently flips the pages of the outdoorsman magazine before throwing it to the floor.

A light mounted on the ceiling tile catches Riley's attention. It shines blue and a chime rings out every five seconds. The sound is insistent but pleasant and Riley knows that someone must be dying somewhere.

The doctor comes into the room and washes his hands briskly under the tap without greeting Riley or Double Al. The nurse who led them into the back room pulls out a blood pressure cuff and rolls up a sleeve on Riley's plaid work shirt. He winks at Riley before pumping away at the black bulb attached to the sleeve.

"What've we got?" the doctor asks as he shakes the water on his fingers to the floor. He snaps on white exam gloves. Riley wonders if they're latex or nitrile. The sight of them reminds him of the nitrous he'd be given before his old dentist would pull his baby teeth. "It's your foot that's the problem?"

"Might be my foot," Riley says and grins at Double Al, "but could be inattention to detail."

The doctor doesn't laugh or warn Riley he's about to swing his leg up onto the table. Riley swears under his breath at the sharp shock brought on by the motion. The doctor walks to a drawer and pulls out a large metal tool that looks better suited for cutting wire or shearing sheep.

"Let's get that boot off and take a look. You want to tell me what happened?"

Riley's eyes dart toward Double Al. He doesn't want to say too much, get his boss and his old family friend in trouble. Of course he's not looking to sue; years of contract law and application of just the right diction and wording to dominate any situation has taken away his stomach for the game. It's certainly a game he won't play against someone he actually respects.

"Worksite miscalculation," is all Riley will give the ER doctor.

Doctor Lemic cuts down the back, front and sides of the boot, sectioning it so it can splay open like a flower with heavy, droopy petals. The nurse helps peel back the layers of leather and the doctor lifts the toe of the boot gently away from the foot and places the sodden mess on a tray behind him.

Riley keeps his face turned away from the mangle he knows is there. He watches Double Al stand up from the chair, his eyes wide and white against his dark complexion. The doctor clicks his tongue, makes a sound of displeasure. Riley can feel the blood that had been contained by his boot slide down his ankle and trickle into the pit of his knee as the doctor keeps his foot hiked high into the air. He wonders how ashen his skin is on his body. He wonders if he could be mistaken for a ghost.

"Oh, buddy," the doctor says and Riley forces himself to look.

The foot itself, the heel, the instep, the ball, is a mass of swollen black and blue punctuated by small swatches of skin still their normal white. But his toes are not right. His toes can't even be rightfully named toes anymore. Five pulpy, bloodied digits hang off his foot. He can see bone protrude out of three of the bits of meat. The bile creeps back up his throat, but not due to the pain this time. Due to the view.

The doctor snaps one of his exam gloves at the wrist and tsks again at Riley like the mess of his toes are his fault. Riley accepts it is his fault, but doesn't like be chided all the same. He wishes he had some nitrous right now, so his mind could be jumbled, his chest prone to heaving with sighs, and there would be no cares to give over his demolished foot.

"Those," says the physician as he looks at what remains of Riley's left toes, "are all going to have to come off."

06   PEACH

She doesn't cuddle after sex and this makes Linx pouty before he drifts off to sleep, oblivious to the sheepskin keeping his legs extra warm. Peach feels mentally energized from the sex but she doesn't want to get out of bed. If Linx feels the mattress lift and her weight depart, he'll stir and then whatever time she would have for thought would be gone.

Digging around in the drawer of her bedside table she produces a Mars bar. She opens the wrapper with her incisors and takes a nibble of the chocolate, a string of caramel left hanging off her front teeth. She could only find the confection at Walmart and she cringed each time she had to go to the store and walk the aisles under the fluorescent lights of Americana. But she did it for the candy. It was necessary.

She puts the chocolate down and picks up the book she began reading a few days back, a John Carter novel entitled *The Gods of Mars*. Her favorite part of the story isn't really the science fiction, the escape scenes, the romance. Her favorite part of the story is the frame surrounding the tale of John Carter and his return to Barsoom, the planet typically known as Mars. It's the story of Edgar Rice Burroughs and his claim that his chronicle is a true account of actual deeds. She delights in Burroughs's way of meta-storytelling, putting himself in the fiction while trying to import John Carter and the denizens of Mars into reality. Plus, the man had a link to Idaho and she feels very connected to her home of Boise, the lava rock-strewn steppes outside the city and the brown mountains to the north. Reading his work makes her feel connected to where she is and reading about Mars makes her feel connected to where she might be going.

There are times Peach feels like her life has been a piece of fiction. Until now. Until this point in time when she's committed to bringing the *real* Peach into existence.

The bloodstone pendant rests on her chest. She pulls the sheet over her bare breasts and puts the book, pages down, on her stomach. Eyes closed, she listens for the calm breathing of Linx indicating he's long past waking. She lets her mind float about. She thinks of those painful skinned knees when she was a child, the meat pocked with sand and tiny rocks around her patellas. She thinks of her first try at making love when she was nineteen, how painful it was not just physically but in the deep muscle of her heart. All the memories would become stories now, *were* already stories, and the present would become a story, too. The only reality Peach desires is the reality of the future. In the future, she would move from her own fictionalizing to facts.

Peach lies in bed for hours, thinking, watching tracers of light zoom around the backdrop of her closed eyelids, the blood running through the thin membrane creating a crimson screen upon which to watch the floaters and the strange shapes. She dozes for a bit and then snaps awake and picks back up her wondering about it all. And about what it would take for her to become bona fide.

07   RILEY

They tell him he's lucky he didn't lose more blood with the extent of the trauma to his foot. All the same, they'll have to amputate the toes quickly to combat the forces of gangrene and its partner, blood poisoning. Riley has no ability to logically protest the cutting off of five of his toes. It's lose them, or lose his life, and while the thought of checking out from his downward spiral is tempting, it's not powerful enough to make him go to his casket all because of a desire to have a full set of toes.

He is prepped for surgery and the last memory he has is of an attractive anesthesiologist entering the room. She has bow-shaped lips and golden eyeshadow and Riley finds himself aroused and not ashamed at the response of his cock. He doesn't wonder if it will calm down by the time he's through surgery. He just stares into the doctor's eyes and thinks about the one instance in which he watched amputee porn. The woman in the film was missing both legs, sliced clean from her body right under her pelvic bone.

"I want you to tell me all your pets' names, starting with last pet and working toward your first," the anesthesiologist says, placing an oxygen mask over Riley's mouth and nose. He answers her, muffled responses through the mask. He begins with the chocolate lab he had when he was in his early twenties, the one that liked to catch squirrels and hold them in his front paws without killing them. Harlequin. But then he's in the black of stopped consciousness before he can speak another name.

What seems to be a second later to Riley has been over two hours to those awake. He comes to in a recovery room, nurses swarming in and out with tubes of liquid and rolls of gauze. The hot anesthesiologist is absent and he can feel the effects of the anesthesia in his system. The room spins while he lies in his hospital bed and his stomach ripples with nausea.

Riley shouts twice for Harlequin. He doesn't realize the dog is long dead before he starts to cry.

The surgeon who removed his toes comes into the room and pulls a clipboard from the base of Riley's bed. He flips some papers around and puts a hand on Riley's good leg. His touch is stabilizing, warm, and Riley does his best to stop his weeping. But he finds it difficult to keep the tears at bay. They're marshaled on by the drugs in his system.

"You're going to heal nicely, Mr. Wanner," the surgeon says. He's an older man with white hair slicked close to his scalp and a pink polo shirt poking up from under his white doctor's coat. "Some recovery time in the hospital and then some physical therapy to help you regain your balance and you'll never know you're missing those toes."

Riley gets his sniffling under control but the water flows steadily out his eyes. He forgets Harlequin and his captive rodents for a moment and remembers why he's in the hospital. And suddenly, because of his taxed emotions and chemicals in his blood, the cause for his trauma is more nefarious than a broken link in a chain.

"Someone's trying to kill me, doctor," he says between heaves of his chest. "It wasn't an accident. There are forces, universal energies, trying to kill me. I had it too good for too long. My happiness is over, doctor. Life wants me dead."

The surgeon puts down the chart and moves around to Riley's side. He puts a hand to Riley's forehead, less out of medical practice than bedside comfort. "It's the drugs they gave you to knock you out, Mr. Wanner. You're completely safe. No one is trying to kill you."

And the tears keep coming. Riley squeezes his eyes shut to try and halt the water but the tears push past his eyelids, leaving his eyelashes damp and soft. He remembers the anvil now, how it was his fault it fell. He thinks of Harlequin, dead at five years, her inexhaustible energy propelling her in front of a maroon minivan.

He feels like he's in her body now. He imagines the heat of summer asphalt under his foot pads and the scent of musky squirrel on his moist nose. He knows he's the only one trying to kill himself. He knows he will unconsciously keep running in front of cars, anvils, pain. No matter if he keeps calling his own name, trying to get himself back to safety, trying to get himself to just stop.

08 PEACH

She blows on Linx's face to wake him. His eyes flutter open and meet her hazel irises. "Get up," she says. "You can't stay over. I've got chores to do."

Linx yawns and looks at the watch on his wrist. His back is damp and the sheet underneath him wet with sweat. "Peach, it's ten at night. Let me stay. I was sleeping well without my Ambien."

"I would," she says, sliding out of bed and putting back on her soft jeans, "but you know the rule. I'm just sticking to what we've agreed to do."

Linx grumbles something about dreaming of dead livestock and sits up. Peach takes in his soft face and his olive skin and a circular dent in his cheek from where he slept on his watch. He can't stay, even if she didn't have things to do. It was something they'd decided on months ago, when they started sleeping together. Both of them thought if they kept the intimacy to a minimum, and this meant sleepovers as well as dates and displays of public affection, they could handle the fuck-buddy status. Peach found herself enforcing the rule more than Linx, which only made sense, given her desire to be anything but his girlfriend.

He leaves her apartment with his shirt on backwards, cardigan unbuttoned and his hair sticking up in a flurry of cowlicks and dry, flaking gel. He doesn't hug her goodbye but gives a flippant wave with his hand as he shuts the door behind him.

Peach watches him leave from the window near her desk, his blue Vespa stalling once before he gets out of the parking lot and on the main road. As he drives away, the apartment complex lights illuminate his departure. She wonders how the cold doesn't cut through him, his torso jacketless, his figure seemingly transported out of some chic European capital.

She peels off her wig and scratches her scalp with her fingernails, running down the middle of her head and down her neck over and over with both hands. It is the motion of separating strands of wet noodles or digging through shag carpeting for a lost earring. Moving to her bedroom, she opens the bathroom door and peers in at the hairy mess she has yet to clean and decides it can wait. She's anxious to get started on another project.

Digging in the back of her clothes closet, Peach pulls forth a dark green duffel bag. It is new to her but second-hand and smells faintly of warming ointment used on achy joints. There isn't much tucked away in it, but she opens it all the same and verifies the contents before zipping it back up.

She takes a hooded sweater out of a chest of drawers and puts it on. It's charcoal gray and made of wool, the fabric sherpa-lined with cream-colored fluff. She brings the hood over her bald head and pulls the strings tight to secure it to her scalp. The wool fibers cause her bare neck to itch but she represses the urge to scratch.

In the kangaroo pocket of the hoodie is a red kerchief. She rubs at a corner of the cotton with her thumb and forefinger and picks up the duffel bag with her other hand. She stops in the small foyer of her apartment to put on dark runners.

When she opens the door, she's reminded of the season. It's below freezing and dark, the cooing of a mourning dove coming from somewhere far overhead on a length of telephone wire. Peach wonders if it looks as though she's going out for a run. It was a strange outfit to wear for a run and an odd bag to carry. But she decides if she is stopped and questioned by some curious neighbor or late-night wanderer, she will tell them she is aiming to run. She's running.

She closes the door behind her. Running. It brings a smile to her lips.

Peach hates to run.

09 RILEY

In his dream he's running the 400 meter at Timberline High
School. His feet seem to skim the slightly bouncy track. His
heels touch earth first, followed by a rolling to the ball of his foot
before shooting off again with his toes as miniature springs. He
wins the race, coming in just before his best friend Walker, a pair
of teal legwarmers around his calves and a girl with pale eyes
and blonde hair holding a cluster of blue balloons. His mother is
waiting for him at the finish line with a juice box and a ham
sandwich.

"You're going to lose," she says, embracing him when he
comes to a stop.

Riley's eyes fly open, his mind awake, returning to the
present in the hospital room. The room is dimly lit. A light from
the nursing station outside shines across the foot of his bed. He
can hear people outside. A cluster of nurses exchange stories and
one of the nurses greets each ending anecdote with a shrill laugh.
Riley looks down at the IV in his arm. He flexes his forearm and

he can feel the shaft of thin plastic buried within his flesh.

He feels back to normal emotionally, the anesthesia leaving his system, helped along by the saltines and Sprite he had before falling asleep. He watches the slice of light grow and shrink on his blanket with the opening and closing of doors outside his room and the movement of the nurses. He guesses at their weight based on how much light they keep off his bed in their passing. He notices while they're illuminated, how his feet both point skyward. His right foot pitches the sheet and blanket up high, the fabric sloping downwards an inch or so to his left foot. The silhouette is of a sloping hilltop bare of tree or radio tower.

Emboldened, Riley flings back the starched sheets and blanket and takes in his amputation. His left foot is swaddled in white bandaging, the end of his foot rounded and stumpy. He looks like a partially-wrapped mummy. A blush of rusty red lines the top of the gauze, blood seeping from his wound.

He can't sense his toes at all. If phantom pains ever were to arrive, they would develop with time. He's grateful his entire leg is numb and dead. A reprieve from the pain is welcome.

The dream returns to his attention. His friend Walker hadn't gone to high school with Riley and the woman must have been some construct of his tired mind. He recalls his mother with the ham sandwich. She wasn't wearing her glasses, too large for her thin nose, and her hair had been straight, not its actual wavy brown. He looks at his mangled foot hidden by sterile dressings and remembers how she used to play *This Little Piggy* with all his toes. She'd finish with one set and move right on to the other. His favorite, and hers, was the little toe on each foot. Instead of the traditional "weee, weee, weee, all the way home," his mother would say, "yippee, yippee, yippee all the way home!"

But she was dead now. As were his toes.

A nurse comes in the room, a caffeine-free soda cradled in one hand and crackers in the other. He has the morose feeling the sweet bubbly drink is the only liquid he will ever drink again.

The salty squares are the only things he will ever eat again. She sighs as she sets down the food on a swivel tray attached to the bed and flips the sheets and blanket back over Riley's legs.

"No need to look at it now," she says and rips open a packet of Saltines. "It'll be there in the morning."

10   PEACH

She beats the dawn back to her apartment. But just barely.
Her neighbor, a woman in her early sixties who lost her husband
years ago, is sipping steaming coffee on her small slab of a
concrete porch. Her hair is in a sharp bob, the strands a mix of
silver and black. Peach notes whenever she sees her, she always
has it coiffed even though Peach has never seen the woman
entertain friends or gentlemen. Her face is flat and heart-shaped
and Peach hazards she's of Inuit descent.

She squints to take in Peach in her dark clothes and hooded
sweater. "You been partying?" she asks Peach, never using her
name.

She's told the woman several times her full name, but she
doesn't seem to remember. When she does venture a guess it's
typically Eileen or Randi. Peach pulls the hood tight around her
chin and nods her head up and down and thinks of something
base and typical to quip.

"I say if you can't do shots on a Monday night, you're too

boring to live."

The woman tucks her feet back underneath the patio chair she sits in and snuggles down into her housecoat. "Got a spare drop for my coffee? Might help me find the Sandman."

"Sorry," Peach says and digs for her apartment keys in the pockets of her hoodie. "Left it all behind me." She smiles at the woman, thinks of her name, Mona, with connotations both sultry and aged. But her neighbor can't see her grin in the dark before dawn, her little patio light casting a slice of yellow only over the dark gray of the concrete.

"You get your rest, then," Mona chides like a mother and takes a sip of coffee. "One of us should be asleep at this hour."

Peach keeps her grin and tries not to think of why only one of them and not both should be in the embrace of slumber. "Will do," she answers.

Keys found, Peach heads inside and leans against her door to shut it. The smile is etched on her face. Her mouth is turned up so high her cheeks begin to ache.

She drops the duffel bag in the entranceway and moves toward her kitchen. Her stomach is jittery from the adrenaline flowing through her system. Her night out was a complete success, devoid of complications or unforeseen challenges. Peach feels like a winner, which is a feeling she's never been blessed with having before.

Her fridge yields up a can of guava juice and she downs the tart liquid in one solid swig, dribbling a bit of the pink juice off her bottom lip due to her inability to cease smiling. She eats handfuls of stale popcorn without salt she popped days ago and forgot about, leaving the bowl out on the counter. Pacing the room, she stops once to flick on the light over the kitchen sink and then resumes walking back and forth across the smooth floor.

The popcorn and juice don't sit well and she stops at the sink, leans over it with her fingers wrapped around the edge of the Formica. She vomits, the adrenaline refusing the food in her system and she tries not to laugh while she pukes pink puffs of corn into the metal sink. Cupping her hand, she washes out her mouth, all the while smiling.

Then she notices the marks. On the refrigerator door handle, the kitchen light switch, the countertop. She can see everywhere her hands have been in her apartment. She reaches up and brushes her cheeks and chin with the back of her hand and comes away with flaking color.

Peach takes in her fingertips in the low light of her kitchen. Several of them are discolored and dark at the very tips. It's on her sweater, her jeans. Her body, her home, all spotted with half-moons of crimson color. It's as if red rose petals have been strewn about, defying gravity and never touching the floor.

She washes her hands in the sink, scrubs them with a little nail brush shaped like a hedgehog and laughs and smiles until the sun dares to light up the room.

WEDNESDAY, THE 25RD OF MARCH, 2015

11   RILEY

"Hey, douchebag," says Walker as he strolls through the hospital room door, a leather work satchel crossing his torso, his work suit creased like a ladder across his lower back. Walker Kauffman would have fit in with those young men on Wall Street in the 1980s if he'd been born a few decades earlier. He has ambition and brains and the incessant lust for a good party. But Riley knows what keeps Walker in check is a healthy respect for the law, his own reputation, and the dependable strength of logic.

Riley smirks and pushes himself up in bed. He sets aside the tray of bland whitefish he's been forcing himself to eat. "Tell me you brought me a cheeseburger. Anything that once had a pulse and didn't swim the English Channel."

His best friend, his former coworker, puts his bag down on the floor and grabs the sheet from Riley's legs and gives a pull. The light blue blanket comes away with the thin, scratchy sheets and Walker gapes at his friend's foot.

"At least they didn't cut the entire thing off from the ankle, Rye. Your ass got lucky this time."

"What do you mean *this time*? Have I ever had a body part amputated before? Yeah," Riley says, "I'm a veritable four-leaf clover."

Walker puts both hands near Riley's wound, where the five toes of his left foot used to come together with his foot. He doesn't touch the bandage but he moves his hands around like he's trying to conjure up images in a crystal ball.

"Shit, you're fine. You're using words like *veritable*," he says as he waves about his hands.

"I once was a lawyer, just like you, Walker. I got myself an education," and Riley laughs, thinks of his time in contract law. He's hard pressed to decide what was worse: his sixty hour work weeks manipulating legal jargon to help one party screw over another party or losing his toes. The verdict is still out.

"What the hell are you doing down there? Manipulating energy?"

"Nah, no hippie crap healing. I'm trying to feel how it is to get your toes smashed by an anvil and keep on living life as such a dumb shit."

Riley laughs and can't think of the last time he let himself become unburdened by his own personal struggles. He adores Walker, though he'd never tell his friend this, preferring to let the typical silence of heterosexual male friendship convey what he feels. He's happy to have a familiar face visit him in the hospital, having put in a call to Walker's mobile after his morphine drip had kicked in. Besides Double Al, no one in his life knows what's happened to him. And for now, he's fine with that fact.

"How's the firm? Working on anything good?"

Walker takes his hands away and bends down, rummages around in his leather bag. "I'm guessing you don't want to talk about your traumatic experience then?"

"I'd rather take a break from it."

Walker keeps at his digging and produces a tube of lip balm he smears on thick before continuing his search. "Nah, nothing to give me a boner. I've got a client who wants to create a legal contract with his thirteen-year-old daughter. If she has sex before being admitted into college, she has to pay her own tuition. Can you believe that crap?"

A nurse pokes her head in the room and Riley smiles and waves her away. She turns and he notices the curves under her navy scrubs. He's feeling better already.

"I can believe it. Hey, think you can pick me up on Friday? I'll be good to go home by then."

"Sure," Walker says and holds up an index finger before pulling something flat from his satchel. He stands and Riley sees a card in his grasp. "But you'll only have been in here five days. Is that enough time to heal? Granted, they won't grow back. But still."

His foot twitches and a line of pain zips from his amputation to his kneecap. "Yeah, I'll be fine. Plus, I haven't been working for Double Al long enough to have health insurance. This is all on me. Or what's left of my trust fund."

"Screw that," Walker says and tosses the card on Riley's chest. "Worker's comp, Rye. I'll be damned if you have to pay a dime on this tab."

The envelope is mustard yellow, bigger than a usual envelope, square and textured. "This get-well-soon card from you?" he asks Walker.

"No. I stopped by your house before coming over to check on the mail. It was the only thing not a flyer or a bill. Thought it might be something capable of cheering you up about your gnarly foot. Like a check for a billion bucks or the best porn in the whole world. Whatever that would look like."

Riley picks it up. It feels like there's cardstock inside. He tucks it under the plate of sodden broccoli and under-seasoned cod. "I'll read it later. Tell me more about work."

Walker plops down on the hospital bed. Riley grimaces at the motion on his foot but keeps smiling.

"There's a new intern," begins Walker, "and I plan on bagging her in two, maybe three months. She has the smallest teeth I've ever seen. Things are like white Tic Tacs but the rest of her is all right."

"I sometimes miss Johnses, Mikelson and Rhodes," Riley says as he ventures another bite of fish. It's worse than before. But like an idiot, he keeps trying.

12   PEACH

"What is it you expect to get out of this counseling session, Peach?"

Camille Swenson sits with her legs crossed and tucked under her bottom on an overstuffed chair. The fabric is patterned alternating blue and yellow stripes and it accents the woman's curly ginger hair and tan pantsuit. She's just plugged in an electric warmer for melting scented wax. The room smells like an oatmeal cookie within moments. The licensed clinical social worker looks over Peach, her eyes coming to rest on Peach's feet.

"Great kitten heel on those shoes, by the way," Camille says as she visually caresses the leather with her gaze. "I love something with just a little bit of lift."

Peach twists her ankles to look over the scarlet shoes on her feet. She put them on to feel more confident, sexier, but so far it wasn't working. The high she felt after her night out two days ago had settled into a miasma of self-doubt. She cringes a bit thinking of the number of times she heaved into her kitchen sink after arriving back home. Five times. The red spots of color weren't the only muck befouling her hoodie and her kitchen that night.

Still, Peach was a believer in actions influencing personality. If she wanted more sexual energy, wanted others to think of her as someone with a strong sexual identity, she'd have to fake it until it became real. Of course, this is only one attribute Peach aims to change about herself. Once again, she thinks of fantasy turning into reality.

"Thanks." She pulls her feet back and does her best to look Camille in the eye. If she doesn't, she'll be reminded to do so. "I guess I just need some encouragement today. I need to believe in myself."

"And that's traditionally something you've been unable to do. Why is that?"

Peach can't think of a singular example for her meek approach to life, not at the moment, so she settles for general feelings. She's well aware there are many instances which kept her fearful of self-actualization. "It might be because I've never done anything with my life that makes me think I'm powerful, dynamic. I've only done things that reinforce my use as a doormat."

Camille shifts on her seat and pulls at one of her dangling earrings. Citrine stones set in silver jangle under her earlobe. "And you're done with getting the dirt and crap of the world wiped across your life. Across your ego."

"In a sense," Peach says and breaks eye contact. She looks down at her lap, at her hands. The skin is dry, her right thumbnail broken down to the quick. A dried line of Super Glue keeps the nail together. She scratches off a bit of red pigment from her cuticle.

"That's not the strong answer a confident person would give. You're allowing yourself to fall back into habitual patterns of noncommittal language."

"Okay."

"No," Camille says and reaches out for Peach's hands. She gives them to the woman but rolls her eyes. "Now you're simply agreeing with me. What is it that you want, Peach?"

There's a clock in the corner of the room. A squat, golden thing with a pendulum for keeping time. It ticks steadily, loudly. Peach narrows her eyes at it.

"I want to break that sorry excuse for a clock. It looks like it was a retirement gift when you left the real estate business in 1983."

A snort comes from Camille, then she's giggling, dropping Peach's hands and pinching her fingers tightly around her waist. Her body pitches slightly backward each time her chest heaves with mirth.

"Grabbing your hands was a bit much, wasn't it?"

"I don't know," Peach says, a smile on her lips. "It could come off genuine to someone who doesn't know about your OCD issues with hand washing."

"And I was never in real estate. And I was five in 1983."

Standing up, Peach smoothes back her wig. "I had to say something to break the tension."

Camille wags a finger at Peach. "Because I was getting too close to something. I get it. You don't have to divulge all your secrets today. Our five minutes was about up, anyway."

The clock holds Peach's interest for a moment longer. For an instant, she thinks the object mocks her. Its ticking tells her she does not have the time, the collection of minutes and days, to see to a sufficient change in her personality. She goes to it, lays it flat on its face. The sound is muted.

"Now get out," Camille says, "I've got to get ready for a real client."

Peach opens the door that leads from Camille's office into a hallway of other doors. A man rushes by her, a mess of folders tucked under one arm. A phone rings incessantly from behind one of the closed doors. The waiting room is to the right of Peach. Individuals wait with problems greater than her own, ready to be saved via therapeutic reflection.

"Oh, Peach," Camille shuffles the papers on her desk, finally producing a bright green paperclip. "Just so you know, you really can do anything you want in life. You're special and you know it."

"Okay," she says and flinches as Camille flicks the paperclip at her in retribution for the blasé answer.

Then she leaves the woman's office, turns left down the hallway, unlocks the door of her own office, and faces a cold room, filing cabinets, drawn blinds, and the professional promise to fix everyone but herself.

13   RILEY

It's mid-afternoon when Walker leaves to get back to work at the law firm. Riley, glad for his visit and happy for his departure, finally sinks back onto his bed, exhaustion claiming his body. He's beginning to feel more in his foot, the nerves coming alive with sparkling sessions of hurt when his muscles randomly enter into spasmodic throes. He depresses the button on his morphine drip until it buzzes a warning and will not dope him with any more of the opiate.

He's glad for his one true friendship with Walker. They'd started at the firm at the same time, straight out of law school. His placement had been at the behest of, and due to the social gravitas of, his father. But Walker was quick-witted when it came to career moves and secured an entry level position at the firm on his talents alone. It was no surprise to Riley that Walker was still there, climbing the ranks in power and salary while Riley had already checked out from a life so closely linked to the idea of an American success story. It was an identity he'd stopped craving once he'd distinguished his own desires from those belonging to his father.

Or so he thought. The sight of Walker with his work bag made Riley a bit jealous. Now he was a cripple and would need to weigh his work options yet again. Maybe it wasn't too late for him to get back in the game of law. He'd only been gone for a short time. He could rejoin the proverbial rat race. He might even win it, if he applied himself. It'd be the only race he could win, now.

Riley does something stupid, decides to flex his left foot, just to see how it feels. He screams out and quickly puts a spare pillow over his face, biting into the white pillowcase. It tastes basic, smells of iodine. No nurses come to check on him after he yells. He's glad for it, but also concerned at their lack of attention.

When the throbbing subsides, Riley pulls on the spiral cord attaching the television remote to his bed. He's about to turn on the screen when he spies the dark yellow envelope tucked under his discarded food tray.

He grabs the paper, balances it in his palm. Definitely a card. He flips it over and sees some of the heft comes from a deep red blob of wax. The seal is just off-centered and it has been made with a tool, a press of sorts. He runs his pinkie finger around the inside of the divot. It's rounded, but not completely smooth. Unlike the initials or crests he's seen dipped in wax seals in movies, this is more geometric and obscure.

He rips the corner of the envelope, preserving the seal and pulls out a card. The front of the card displays a picture of a sorrowful, anthropomorphized panda holding a cluster of wilting daisies in its paws. Riley opens the card to see the printed message inside: *Beary Late Than Never. Happy Belated Birthday!*

There's more, written in handwriting that tilts a bit to the left with curly loops for serifs:

Don't you just feel like a wolf in sheep's clothing sometimes? At least you aren't the black sheep of the family. Sorry I missed your birthday, but it wasn't the right time to wish you well just yet. I'm looking forward to Lucky Number 8!

Love,

Hamal

Riley reads the card two more times, trying to make sense of its contents. He's not sure, but he thinks he had a thought about being a wolf in sheep's clothing before the anvil slipped to the floor to squat on his foot. He flips over the envelope. There's no return address, but his home address is written in the same distinctive handwriting. His birthday was nearly a month ago and the only mail he'd gotten then was a simple drawing of a fenced pasture containing cows and a large, man-sized golden eagle from five-year-old Tate Marchesi. The kid with the greenish-brown eyes and raspy chuckle could be his biological child, though Riley and his ex-girlfriend Kristin have both avoided the work of deciphering his parentage for a certainty.

He doesn't know a Hamal and has no idea what *lucky number 8* refers to. Nor does he care.

His foot twinges, pain rushing up to his stomach. He presses the nurse call button on his bed frame and tosses the card and envelope on the chair nearest to him. He needs some stronger pain killers or an override switch on his morphine drip. And as he looks at the gloppy wax on the envelope, he decides he could use some cherry Jell-O, too.

14   PEACH

     She walks to her office door, finally finished with her clients for the day, and clicks the lock on her doorknob. The idiom *herding cats* comes to mind and she decides it isn't descriptive enough to sum up what she does at her job. Cats would be manageable if for nothing more than the sheer predictability of cats. They will either purr and rub or hiss and attack. But it will be one of those options. Each day her clients stymie her with new problems, neuroses and poor choices.

     If only she worked with cats instead.

     Peach plunks back down into her swiveling desk chair and sighs. Her head has been itching all day and scratching through the wig does little to give her relief. She doesn't dare remove her wig; she's grateful she's spent two days coming to work with no one, not even Camille, the coworker she's closest to, commenting on any difference in her looks.

     She puts her elbows on her desk, reaches her hands up behind her head and slips her fingers under the tight netting at the base of her skull. Here, where her neck meets her head is the point of annoyance. She runs her nails against her scalp. Her hair has always grown slowly; the long tresses had taken her years to cultivate. Her new locks haven't broken through the skin yet but she knows in a few days, she'll be dealing with the itch of sharp follicles pushing through the dermis like grass pushing through a garden bed.

She scratches away happily, closing her eyes. She pictures herself as a super heroine, decked out in a shimmering red cape, bodice, boy shorts. Instead of a big P on her chest, there's an S and it doesn't stand for *super*. It stands for *self*. She wants nothing more than to conquer her identity, to subdue it, change it. Turn it to steel. Use it for a life of epic note.

For now, she scratches happily. She works away the itch that lives right where the reptilian brain comes to dally with the cerebrum. Where primal meets refined. It's also one of the weakest parts of the skull, tenuous in strength. It's a point of weakness for all humanity. It's Peach's greatest bridge to gap.

Before she rouses herself from her thoughts to head home and work on other tasks, she pulls a small lighter from the long drawer where she keeps her pens and staples and coins for the soda machine in the front foyer of her office building. It's a brass Zippo she found on a walk along the Boise River last month. It had been the first day of warmth in 2015 and she'd seized the opportunity to meander outside before the afternoon brought a set of snow flurries, each one worse than the last, winter reminding her it was not yet done with her city.

She rubs her thumb against the flint wheel and watches the butane flare. A triangular flame dances around above the brass casing and she thinks to run a finger through it, to feel the heat and mimic those badasses she's seen in movies who pass their flesh through small flames to show they are impervious to pain. But this is no movie and she respects fire too much to taunt it.

In her curiosity to learn how old the Zippo was, she did

some digging online and found out some interesting things about the manufacturer and the lighter's history and role in American society. To be part of a Zippo Squad in the Vietnam War meant you were sent in to burn down a village with nothing more than the lighter in your pocket. She thinks of Linx, his mother Thai, but wonders all the same if any of his relatives were somehow in Vietnam, caught in the burn started by a flint-wheel igniter.

Most people had a healthy fear of fire. If one started, gained speed and intensity, they would flee. Then why, she wonders, did she have the desire to do the opposite?

"I want to run toward you," she whispers down into the flame.

The fire responds by singeing a few strands of her wig, punishment for getting too close. The room smells of scorched carbon. The burnt hair is real, though it isn't biologically hers. But all hair smolders just the same.

FRIDAY, THE 27TH OF MARCH, 2015

15 RILEY

"If I don't get a decent drink by the end of this day, I'm retaining you as counsel and then I'm going to set fire to this hospital."

Walker has his arms outstretched and Riley uses them to steady his wobbly legs. He's standing on his own, though his left foot doesn't support any weight. The pair wait for the nurse to return with crutches. When they pushed in a wheelchair through his hospital room door, Riley told them to take it away. He was resolute on walking out of the hospital.

"And as your counsel I'd be remiss if I didn't tell you you'd be a dumbass to set anything on fire. Not with your luck lately. You're going to be golden if we can just keep you whole and fed, Rye."

"Maker's Mark. Neat."

"You're an alcoholic."

"Sorry, no. Didn't think of booze the entire time I was healing from having my digits cut off. But now I'm free, I'm getting soused."

"Fair enough," Walker says and the nurse with the nice shape and round ass walks in with a pair of crutches. Riley winks at her and she raises an eyebrow.

"So these will cost me, what, seven hundred dollars to take?"

She tucks the cushioned metal under both of his arms and Walker pulls back, gets out of his friend's way. Riley tries them out, keeping his left leg bent at the knee. His balance is a bit shaky but he's only left bed to piss and shit over the past five days.

"Not quite that much, Mr. Wanner," she says with a smile.

Walker swings Riley's bag of personal items over his shoulder. Double Al had been good enough to pick a few things up from his house and drop them off the night he was admitted to St. Al's hospital. He'd been high on the strong doses of opiates that night and when Double Al told Riley he needed to leave for him to get his rest, Riley had shouted at him as he departed. "Saint Al!" he dubbed him. "Saint Al in Saint Al's! It's a springtime miracle. You are the biggest of all the saints."

Riley gets a cadence down with the crutches and moves out of the room, Walker at his side. The nurse passes, glancing at Riley over her sloping shoulder. "That ass of hers is the only thing I'll miss about this place," he mutters.

It takes thirty minutes for the men to get to the parking garage. Walker chatters on about the weather, work, his ex-girlfriend. Riley keeps his focus on his feet, paranoid he'll catch his foot on a parking space block. They arrive at Walker's little Miata and Riley lifts his eyebrows.

"This should be interesting to settle into," he says. Walker mumbles, "that's what she said," under his breath. Riley grins despite the soreness in his armpits from the crutches and the tiredness in his right leg and waits for Walker to unlock the car and pop the passenger side door open. Handing Walker his crutches, he falls back into the bucket seat and winces on impact.

Walker takes the speed bumps slowly as he maneuvers his car out of the garage. Riley braces himself with his hands against the soft roof of the shuttered convertible. Then they pull out onto the road running parallel to the hospital, headed for the Connector, a section of interstate winding through the greater Boise area. Flowering pear trees have exploded with white blossoms while Riley has been in the hospital. His nose catches their cloying, putrid scent when he rolls down his window. The air licks this face, wild and new, nothing like the oxygen he'd been forced to breathe during his convalescence.

They hit a stop light before the on-ramp to the Connector. Riley scoots up on his seat, his eye drawn to a bit of color in the middle of the intersection. There, at the junction of Emerald and Curtis roads, is what looks to be a giant V painted in bright red. The tops of the V curl outwards like shepherd's hooks.

"What the hell is that?" he asks Walker.

"No clue. But they're all over town from what I can see on my drives from work to home and out to play. I think one of the local stations did a piece on it. Just some bored kid tagging asphalt. At the worst, a new gang sign. Does Boise even have gangs? I should know that, right?"

Riley keeps his eyes on the symbol. It settles into his mind. When he closes his eyes and turns his face to the warm sun out his window, he can see it etched in his vision. The force of the fiery ball of hydrogen backlights the figure in burnt sienna. He doesn't realize until they hit the Connector that Walker is going the wrong direction. The Miata zooms toward downtown Boise.

"Uh, house is the other way, Walker."

Walker reaches over to Riley and pushes him on the shoulder. His body slides back down in the bucket seat.

"No shit," Walker says. "I'm not taking you home."

16   PEACH

She typically didn't see clients on Fridays, but she had to cancel some of her regular meetings on Tuesday after the fun she'd had on Monday night. She'd been unable to focus the following day and she could tell her clients sensed her antsy detachment. She was fidgeting with pens, any pen she could get her hands on while they spoke of their current problems or thoughts and she'd flick them against her thighs or her desktop, dreaming of wearing her gray hoodie and going out for a "run." Peach was playing catch up, now, Friday late afternoon, when she should have been working on case reports for the week.

It was small inconvenience she was very willing to bear for her personal development.

She lifts the bloodstone pendant off her chest. Peach rubs the face of the multicolored gem between her fingers and her mind begins to drift back to when she received the necklace as a gift. The voice of the woman who gave her the present replays within her mind. Her English is spoken with a Russian accent.

She listens for her deep voice listing off the stone's metaphysical powers: courage, increased self-esteem, tenacity.

But she doesn't allow her memory to deepen and expand until it pulls her from her office and into her past. She has work to do. She cups her palms around the stone and tries to find her own center, the place in her body where her energy resides and pulsates. She finds it, in the middle of her pelvis, just below her navel. It thumps away, hot, pulling at the nerves in her belly button.

For a time, she stays present with the sensation and keeps her eyes shut tightly. Then she releases the pendant and digs around in one of her desk drawers. She pulls out a small candle, rose-scented, and the Zippo. She flicks the lighter wheel to get a flame and sets the wick ablaze. There is the smallest indent in the wax; she's only burned it a few times before.

She puts her face over the candle, not to the catch the scent of rose, but the first whiff of acerbic smoke from the burning metal in the wick.

Someone jiggles the handle of her door, pushing on it slightly to get in. Peach immediately licks her fingers and pinches out the candle. A drop of hot wax congeals on her finger and she picks up the candle and hides it behind a stack of books on her desk. To Peach, her play with the flame is a ritual unfit for uninitiated eyes.

He's early, but he always is.

Peach tugs at her wig to makes sure it sits square on her scalp and goes to the door. As she unlocks it, a man, thin and tall with bright eyes and a small goatee rushes into the room. He's in his early thirties, just like Peach, and he wears a deep purple cardigan over a threadbare dress shirt. An outline of a small tube shows through the pocket over his chest. The man smells like dirt and the body odor which comes from being outside, at work, in frigid air. His face is stricken, pained. It's not the look of physical pain but of emotional anguish.

"You're early, Michel," Peach says, standing aside for him to sweep into the room and take a seat on the upholstered chair where she directs her patients to sit. It's a gaudy thing of warm-colored flowers made of velveteen material.

"How can you keep me out, *ma chérie?*" The man's face is suddenly aglow. A spark of mischief shows in the upturning of his mouth. "How can you lock out your lover, your ideal for all men on this planet?"

17   RILEY

When they hit Main Street, Riley figures out where they're
going. The white Miata pulls into the parking lot of a building
just outside of the city center. It's early evening and the sun has
yet to make its escape from the sky. But twilight is coming and
soon, the place will come alive with patrons. Men like Riley and
Walker.

Walker pops the parking brake and tosses Riley a smart
grin. Riley keeps his eyes on the building. It's an old, squat
structure with a marquee above the entrance advertizing beer
specials and fifty-cent wings via scrolling lights. The entry door
is padded in a dirty, maroon vinyl, brass studs securing the fabric
to the wood underneath. Coniferous bushes run the length of the
front of the building, their undergrowth polluted with new
dandelions vibrant with yellow blooms and bits of plastic debris
and cigarette butts.

There's a loud pop, a flow of electricity, and a neon sign
flares to life on the roof of the building. The shingles appear to

be alight with blue, white and yellow flames. Their peaked tips all bend toward the east, as if a strong, constant gale bent the glass tubing.

And then the last neon sign comes to life, a bold lettered beacon at the corner of the parking lot. It spells out *Blaze Lounge.*

"Well," Walker says, "I thought you wouldn't mind stopping by your home away from home. You know, to shake off the hospital cobwebs. The gauze webs."

"Trademark that winner right now," Riley teases.

A cluster of men, all wearing ball caps with the bills jutting out over their backs, hoot at a passing car and then move inside the lounge. When they pull open the door, Riley can see the muted black of the inside, punctuated by shocks of laser lights in pink and orange.

He can almost smell the stink of musky body lotion from where he sits in the Miata. He can definitely hear and feel the shaky boom of a subwoofer's bass. He thinks to make a joke about his soul being of the same low frequency but holds back.

"I'm a bit sad you know I'd rather come here than shower and eat some ham and bean soup on my couch," Riley says, finally looking over to his friend. "But I'm only a bit sad. More thankful, really."

Walker flips down his visor and checks on his hair in the mirror, smoothes on a new layer of pineapple-scented lip balm. Riley pulls at the door handle and cracks open his door, placing his good foot, his right foot down on the asphalt. Riley nods to his crutches stretching from the back of the tiny sports car to the front dash. If he wanted to be the responsible, hard-working man Double Al expected him to be, he would rethink a night out to a strip club after having his toes amputated. But if his recent trial had taught him anything, it was to embrace the fun of the present before the future and thoughts of the past destroyed it.

"Grab those, Walker," he says.

Riley grinds his right toes against a flattened foam cup on the asphalt. Parts of the white matter break off and skid away over the parking lot, chunks of glacier turning into solitary, individual icebergs.

"Let's party."

18   PEACH

"We're going to have to wrap this up, Michel. We're over our therapeutic hour and I need to do some paperwork before I can get out of here."

Peach keeps her hands flat against her thighs. It's the only way she can prevent herself from reaching up and scratching at her scalp. Michel cocks his head, presses a finger to his lips.

"You've changed your hair."

Peach sighs. "You're stalling for time, Michel."

The man keeps his finger to his lips, speaks through it like it has been glued there. "You have done something to your hair. A rinse, maybe. You've darkened it. It's a bit redder."

Peach stands, shakes out her hands and pulls at her blouse. Michel is always good at stalling to get more of Peach's time. She knows his attachment to her is unhealthy; he's clearly experiencing issues with transference. He doesn't truly love her; she knows this is a case of misplaced affection toward her because she represents a stable, caring, non-judgmental presence in his life. It's taken her five months to get Michel to even consider his feelings for her might be less than genuine or healthy.

"It's the lighting in here, Michel," Peach quips, then changes the subject. "So anything you want to end with today? We've gone over your goals for the week: checking your paranoid thoughts with reviewing of facts and keeping a log of the times you find yourself self-abusing or self-deprecating, either physically or mentally. Any new thoughts or experiences you'd like to share with me before we end our meeting?"

The thin man moves his finger down to his goatee and strokes it absently. The hair on his chin and his head is chestnut brown in color and there is a black smudge of something under his fingernail. He picks up a knickknack from the bookshelf next to where he sits in the patients' chair. It's a small obelisk made of soapstone. He runs a nail over its surface but it escapes without a scrape. Peach keeps herself from snatching it away, knowing it would only upset him. It was a gift to her, from someone very dear, whom she hasn't seen in years.

He speaks quietly, his focus on the elongated pillar that ends in a sharp point.

"Two things: obelisks were raised in the past to celebrate the achievements of great men or tell stories in pictures to the common folk staring up at their decorated sides. I learned about them in high school AP World History. Also, I've never hurt a woman."

He cups a palm over the point of the obelisk and plunges it again and again into his flesh. Peach doesn't react, doesn't pull it away. She's used to his acting out, his constant desire to bring sensation to his body via physical pain. If she sees blood, she'll stop him.

"You're being too general with your last statement, Michel. We've talked about this before. If you want to talk about specific experiences, that's different."

Peach watches Michel's face. He's brought up his past before like this. Always a nebulous statement of some past wrong, but never a story to back it up. She's aware he has a history of violence, but Peach isn't always sure where Michel's inner world and outer world coincide. She's not even sure he knows what's real and what's not. But then again, Peach struggles with that, too.

He puts down the little statue. Peach doesn't see blood on its tip.

"Not today," Michel says. "But I wanted to remind you. I've never hurt a woman."

It's something he says to her, plies her with each time they have a session. Peach is aware of what he means by the statement. It is less a bit of information to make her feel at ease and more a declaration.

Michel has not hurt women. But that doesn't mean he hasn't hurt men.

Peach knows advertizing this fact is a point of pride for her patient. And though she should curb his boasting, it helps his self-esteem. And without it for a groundwork, she has nothing to build on. If Michel identifies as a violent man, who is Peach to tell him he cannot be such a thing?

She considers coming up with her own slightly perverse statement to say to herself each day. Perhaps it will give her a solid backbone to make the changes she needs to make in her life.

"*Ma chérie*," he whispers, eyes looking at the bloodstone pendant around Peach's neck. She can see he notices she's drifted off in thought and won't give him the satisfaction of asking today about his run-ins with other men.

"The only part of you that's French is your first name," she says, smiles. "And we've talked about the pet names. Let's stick with Peach. I'm not deserving of your attention anyway, Michel. Save it for someone special."

He stands up abruptly at this, nearly knocking over a mug of cold tea at his feet.

"You're the perfect woman. Perfect Peach. I use this name for you when I'm not using *ma chérie*. It's true and you are. Perfect Peach."

She bends, moves the cup away from Michel and does her best not to make eye contact with him. He has the habit of locking in his stare, moving with her as she squirms to break his focus. She keeps quiet, head down as she walks to her office door and pulls it open. Perfect Peach. Perhaps this will become her new mantra, the thing she says to herself over and over.

"I think we've had a great session, Michel. I'll see you next week. Don't have too much fun this weekend, okay?"

Peach keeps her focus outwards on the hallway, her body pointed in the same direction. Michel re-shelves the soapstone pyramidal statue, pats down the front of his cardigan and reaches into his shirt and pulls a single cigarette from the front pocket. He places it in his mouth and lets it dangle unlit from his lower lip.

"Women are better than men, Perfect Peach. They're soft, fragile. Both their bodies and their hearts. They're worth defending and protecting. Not like men. Only the most precious things are breakable, right?"

He holds his place in the office and Peach looks at the wood grain of her office door. It's painted white, but she can see the swirls, gaps and texture of the natural material through the pigment. The random patterning suggests a puppy's face, a cluster of bananas. And near the base of the door is the writhing form of a dancing woman, thick and lush, her hips bumped over to one side. Asking for it.

19   RILEY

It's the third bourbon that makes Riley finally relax into his chair. It's the same chair he always sits in at Blaze Lounge: the one with a view of the entire length of the stage. It's closest to the pole jutting out of the raised walkway. And from here, he watches Nell work.

Nell Hyde, surely a stage name. He doesn't know why she's his favorite stripper. She's a bit stiff when she dances. Her legs seem to always stay rigid. She brings a knee up to hook around the pole and lets her body weight twirl her back down to the stage. But her foot, toenails painted bright blue in a platform heel, stays taut with muscles flexed.

Of course, Riley knows his presence must not be helping the woman relax as she shimmies and lifts her body through the routine set to "Ice, Ice Baby." He's aware Nell dislikes him. She has a sneer reserved for him alone. And this, naturally, makes him want her all the more.

Walker plunks down two more Maker's Marks at the table

and pulls a chair under his butt. "This is the last one. Then I'm cutting you off. Booze and prescription pain killers are an awesome combo. But only when you're not post major amputation."

"I'm totally fine. It's been a few hours since my last oxycodone," Riley says, eyes on the way Nell's top rides up her breasts. He can see the fullness of the underside of her chest slip under the skimpy band of fabric taxed with keeping it all in. He wonders if she has scars where they slipped in the silicone bags. The club is too dark to yield up any clues. "My toes feel great."

"The toes not there anymore? Those are okay? I'm glad," Walker smiles.

Nell finishes her set with a front bend. She grabs and holds her ankles and twerks her ass at the patrons at the bar behind her. Riley misses the view but he notices Nell looking at him while she moves. Her eyes are on his bandaged foot. Her mouth twists, shows her top teeth.

There's ragged applause. Riley doesn't bother with clapping when she lifts herself up and makes for the backroom. Her heavy platforms clack audibly against the hard stage. He can hear Walker yell something, but he's feeling the alcohol now. It feels like there are wads of cotton in his ears.

"Lap dance, sweetie," Walker says and waves a fifty at Nell. "For my boy here with the battle wound. Well, work wound, I suppose."

He stands and proffers a hand to the stripper. She takes it and he helps her down off the stage. She trips on a bit of nothing, an ankle twisting slightly, but Walker catches her right above the g-string at her hips.

"Him?" she asks, pointing to Riley. Her lips flatten, eyes narrow.

"I've missed you, too, Nell," Riley grins. He reaches for his drink and nearly tips it over. A drop or two of amber liquid falls on the sticky table.

"No hands. I remember the first time I danced on you. No repeats of that shit," she says and abruptly turns and hovers over Riley's lap. He knows she's somewhere far away mentally, nowhere near him. Her movements are staid and rehearsed. She hums along with the song playing over the loudspeakers, some poppy bit of fluff that makes pole work easier for the girls. She smells like jasmine and garlic and her dyed, burgundy hair hits Riley's chin.

After a minute, she says something to Riley but he can't catch it with her face turned away and the music blaring. She speaks again, louder, with her neck craned around to see his face.

"What happened to the foot?"

Riley puts his hands on her hips and roughly pulls her down onto his crotch. His dick is hard and he holds her there for a moment before she pries back his fingers and stands up in frustration.

"Life," he says and then smacks her sharply on the ass.

And he knows there are repercussions to his actions. Except he's not manhandled out by bouncers or yelled at by some other staff member. A big, pasty cheeked man wearing small hoops in his earlobes walks over to Riley and pulls Nell toward his chest.

She yields, folds into the man's wide embrace, and smirks at Riley.

"Ah, the boyfriend! The savior. The dude who plays at being muscle when he's nothing more than a creepy stalker."

Sev wrinkles his nose, speaks with a noticeable Australian accent. "My girlfriend, my ass."

Walker watches the exchange from his seat. Sev pushes Nell away and hovers over Riley with his mass. He wears a beat-to-shit black leather duster and a set of fingerless gloves on his hands. He drops a bar napkin in Riley's lap and walks away, back to his barstool and a waiting bowl of red-skinned peanuts.

The napkin blows off his legs and under his seat due to the revolutions of an overhead fan. He fishes it back, sure to not put weight on his left foot, and squints to make out the few lines written there. The man's handwriting is all caps, heavily inked and more squat than elongated. There are a few holes where Sev pushed too hard with his pen and ripped through the white napkin. He reads it once and hands it to Walker. Walker snorts, reads it aloud.

"Dark waste blooming, sinews snapped. We are monsters."

Riley picks up his whisky and tips it in Sev's direction. The only acknowledgement he gives Riley is a set of raised middle fingers.

"Fucker is a poet," Riley says.

20   PEACH

By the time she leaves the blue-green, three-story office building, dark has closed in on the day and the solitary croak of a frog escorts her to her car parked in the attached asphalt lot. Peach thinks it's a bit early for the amphibians to be waking up, but this spring has turned warm in the last few days and the earth begins to thaw, readily pliant and fresh. No doubt the frog came back to life early, resurrected from his hibernation under an awning kept from harsh winds or a pile of decaying leaves.

Her attention is on the throaty rumble of the frog when Michel steps up next to her. She has her car keys in hand as always. It's her poor plan for self-defense when she leaves work late and she's not really surprised she doesn't think to rake the jagged metal of her keys down his arm and run. Peach isn't a natural fighter. She simply turns and faces him, resigned.

"You're amazingly quiet," she says and leans her back against her car door window.

"I've learned it doesn't ever pay to be too loud. Sneakier is better. Silent is best."

"Okay," Peach says and puts her hands in the air. "I give up, Michel. What do you want me to say? All the clichés? I don't think it would work. We're not a good fit. It's not you, it's me. You only think you love me. Shall I go on?"

"One date with me," Michel whispers. He doesn't press in closer to Peach, careful to keep his body from touching hers. She tries not to think how long he's been waiting for her outside. Hours of waiting could be considered stalking, but she has no desire to escalate the situation. While she trusts he has never harmed a woman, there is nothing stopping him from starting today.

"How about this one? You're just not my type." She softens her delivery with a smile.

"You don't like your men crazy?"

"I wouldn't say that," Peach hedges, "but you aren't crazy, Michel. We all need a little help sometimes."

Michel tilts his head and digs in his front pocket for his cigarette. She looks at the thing: Camel, filterless. He puts it in his mouth.

"You never light it, do you?" Peach asks.

"Course not. Then what? I'd just have to find another."

Peach can't fault his logic. And she finally decides to chance a look into his eyes. He has short lashes, but they're thick and dark and his right cheek is punctuated with a sole dimple. She feels blood rising to her face and she breathes deeply. He's cute, but no matter what she says to Michel's face, he is certainly crazy.

And there is the other matter which complicates things.

He keeps his dark eyes on hers and she knows she'll have to turn away from him soon.

"I just don't think dating you would be appropriate," she quips. She settles into his stare just a bit. She takes it as a challenge to keep breathing under stressful conditions.

"Because of the therapist and patient relationship?"

"What?" Peach is thrown for a moment. She hadn't been thinking of their professional arrangement, but of course it would be the obvious reason not to engage in a romantic relationship with Michel. It was the most obvious reason to him and so Peach needed to go with it. He could never know the most obvious reason for her. At least, not yet.

"Yes, right. The completely wrong thing to do."

And then she finally turns around and unlocks her door. She's not afraid to have her back to him. She instinctively knows he'll never attack her, grab her, and overpower her. And Peach is grateful for this feeling of safety with Michel. It makes her desire to change herself that much easier. Because she'll have one less worry in the future

"I'll see you next week," Peach says as she slips into her car and shuts the door. She does not lock it, afraid it would hurt his feelings.

Michel removes the cigarette from his mouth. He wipes the end of it on his purple cardigan and puts it back in his shirt pocket. His answer is muffled by the metal and glass between them.

"I'll see you tonight in my bed, *ma chérie*. Dreams and dreams and dreams of a ripened Peach."

21   RILEY

"I think my dick got harder when I noticed her flabby wall of a boyfriend watching us from the bar."

Walker shifts his Miata down a gear and pulls into Riley's driveway. Little solar lights dot the walkway up to his front door, put in by the landscapers he'd hired when he first bought the house. A tall shock of yellow forsythia flowers shines in the dark against the stone façade of his house's entryway.

"You're drunk as hell, Rye. And I'm going to be late for my date if I don't get you out of this car in ten minutes."

Riley drops his head back against the bucket seat and whines. "Why'd you make a date tonight? It's not even ten o'clock yet. I could have had more to drink and another dance or three."

"You could have gotten your nose broken by the poet. You've just had major surgery, brother. You don't have ten toes anymore. Can you just have a night in to heal up and chill out?"

"Says the guy who took me to Blaze Lounge. I'm fine,"

Riley says. "Stay here and we'll play darts."

"Go to bed," Walker says and gets out of the car. He walks around to Riley's door and tries to open it. But Riley makes a game out of locking and unlocking the door, laughing as Walker tries to time his pulling on the handle with Riley's slowed movements. He wins out and flings back the metal, the hinges squeaking in protest.

"You're lame when you get this drunk. Up and out."

Riley steadies himself with hands on the dashboard. The world spins but his foot is limp and numb. "I'm thirty-one, Walker. And I have nothing."

Walker pulls Riley out by his elbows and gets him propped up on his crutches. Riley can smell his own body odor as he lifts his arms and promises himself a shower if he can shake off his drunk and get a plastic bag over his foot.

"Nothing. Right. Not this huge house behind me. Not a nice financial cushion when your parents died even though you've systematically blown most of it. Not enough strange to keep you visiting the free clinic until you've retired. Okay, Rye."

The crutches wobble underneath him, but Riley manages to keep upright. His mouth is devoid of moisture and his fingers feel swollen.

"But only five toes. And failures."

"So you're human," Walker says and pushes Riley to start walking.

"But not a real man," Riley says and plants his right foot solidly on the brick pavers that line his driveway. "Real men have sex with whomever they want, when they want. So I'm going to bypass dickface Sev and fuck Nell. That's my goal. Screw going back to work or succeeding in life. I'm going to plow that stripper."

Walker nudges Riley on his back to get him started for his door, but he doesn't budge. His best friend tosses his hands in the air and shakes out the light brown hair shellacked to his head.

"So you're going to devote your energy to pursuing sex with a woman who openly detests you? And it will be your life's focus? Really?"

Riley doesn't speak but nods his head yes.

Walker gets back in his car, turns the ignition and rolls down the window. He rubs a stick of lip balm against his lips and returns the small tube to his pocket. "Get inside, idiot. Sober up and get a better goal."

He pulls away, off to his date and Riley stands, shaky from exhaustion and too much booze, no desire to make it inside his empty house even though the night is cool enough to make him shiver. One of the solar-powered lights at his feet blinks off, all the energy it'd harnessed from the sun spent, used to illuminate nothing.

22   PEACH

Another man is waiting for her when she gets home to her apartment. She puts on a forced smile when she sees Linx loitering on her little porch. He has a six-pack of a microbrew at his feet and a white bag in his hands. Grease soaks through the paper.

"Thought fried chicken sounded good," he says and leans in for a little peck on Peach's cheek.

She wants to tell him to leave. They didn't have plans to hang out, but she can't bring herself to say no to him, the task made harder by his gentle, earnest nature. And it isn't special treatment for Linx. All her denials and refusals are polite and malleable. If anyone tries hard enough to reverse her decisions, she'll likely cave. And this is a part of herself she plans on killing off. No more yielding Peach.

"You're a vegetarian."

"Good for you," Linx says and follows her inside after she unlocks her door. "All the chicken goes on your dish. I'd be the best boyfriend. I'm considerate. And I even share my beer."

She wrinkles her nose at his offer to share his alcohol and watches as he puts the grease-soaked bag down in the kitchen and pulls a plate from the cupboard over the stovetop. Linx looks at Peach. She holds her cheeks in her palms, just briefly, trying to cradle away the exhaustion she feels.

"Are you okay? I should have offered to take you out to a nice dinner. Somewhere they don't let kids in. Or if they do, they can't color on the tablecloths."

"I'm okay, Linx. Just tired. I wasn't expecting company tonight."

He doesn't bite at her insinuation. Instead, he rambles off a list of Boise's nicest restaurants and promises to take her to one next weekend. He always knows what's hottest on the dining scene, working in the food service industry himself.

She lifts her face away from her hands and swallows. "I can't next weekend. I'll be busy." She tries her best to calm the quiver she thinks she hears in her voice. She wants to act nonchalant.

"Then tomorrow night. No excuses."

"But it's not a date, Linx. Right?"

He flicks his flat chest with his thumbs and index fingers, his way of playing coy. "No, not a date."

Popping a top off one of his IPAs, Linx heads into the living room. He flips on the television and spends several minutes perusing channels until he settles on something with ballroom dancing and commentators.

She's glad he's distracted himself. Peach isn't up to playing invested friend for the evening. She snatches a heavier coat hanging off a chair at her kitchen table and puts it on.

"I'm going outside for a minute. Then I'll be back for the chicken."

Linx waves a dismissal at her, engaged with a couple in matching attire swinging across the screen. Both dancers are bedazzled in copper sequins and feathered headdresses.

She hopes to hear another frog when she closes the door behind her, but there are never the sounds of croaks near her apartment. Too much concrete. So she walks behind her apartment to a grassy common area between three separate buildings which house six apartments each.

Using her hand, she tests the cold grass for dampness before sitting down and pulling her knees up to her chin. Peach stares at the sky. The moon has yet to rise, but the light pollution from her neighborhood kills the brilliance of the stars overhead.

But she's patient. And as she looks up, her eyes focus on the points of white beginning to pierce the ambient light and make their own light known to the woman sitting on the chilly earth. The stars come out like wary survivors of a war, passing through haze and obscurations to state their existence to someone, anyone. Peach is that someone. She thinks of it as a blessing.

She presses her fingertips to her lips and blows kisses to the universe, picking out the stars she knows by name and flinging them her love and devotion. But the faraway sun she cherishes most isn't in the night sky right now. She'll have to wait until long after the heat of summer leaves Boise to see it hang in the black expanse overhead for longer than an hour after sunset. By then, the star will be poised high, parallel to the North Star, but Peach will be enamored with another star. But this is how it will work. Heavenly, burning bodies taking turns at having importance to Peach.

"I want to be different. Give me strength, give me the courage to make the transformation. I want to be the true Peach. As Michel says, Perfect Peach. I want to take what's owed me. I want to shine!"

She talks to the one star she desires to see shining, speaking to it in its absence, until Linx comes out to find her, a plate of lukewarm chicken in his hand. The stars tell her he's coming long before she sees his shadow walking across the hilly ground to where she sits. They give her enough time to be silent and act as if they'd not been conversing.

The stars tell her many things. Except whether or not she'll be able to get what she wants out of life. That's the mystery they keep from her. But she understands the game.

"I'm famished," she tells Linx. He offers her a hand up and they walk in silence back to her home. She thinks, while they walk over the grass awakening from its winter respite, there could be all manner of living creatures slumbering underneath her feet. They would not know of her or her ability to shine.

Regardless, she still beams.

23 RILEY

He notes the way his house smells when he's been away from it for a few days. When everything is closed up and fresh air isn't allowed inside, the place gets musty thanks to a broken air conditioner line that spewed water into his crawlspace last summer. He sneezes, hobbles around on his crutches to open up windows. With each pane of glass he slides up, a frigid cascade of air pours into the room. He stands in front of the window in his guest bedroom, having half-skipped his way upstairs, and lets the cold night breeze smack him in the chest.

He has a retro style rotary phone on the bedside table in the guest room. Riley takes a step toward the bed and when he's a few feet away, he leans the crutches against the side of the mattress and pitches forward, throwing himself face down on the fluffy comforter. He turns his head, blows his shaggy, blond hair out of his eyes and thinks about picking up the phone.

It's midnight. And while one of the people he wants to call might still be awake, the other certainly isn't. Besides Double Al and Walker, there are only two others who mean a thing to him. And he reasons he should tell them about his amputation and the falling anvil. But he knows it can wait until morning, or another day when he's not tipsy from too many fingers of Maker's Mark.

Toes and fingers, fingers and toes.

He clenches his fists tight and relaxes them. Over and over. Blood rushes to his hands and they heat up, solid, warm flesh rebelling against the chilly air of the room. The bedspread is soft from years of use. It's made of gray and black fabric, with a faded pattern of geometric shapes along the sides. His dad went with him to pick out the comforter before he went away for his freshman year of college. Riley had liked the somber colors and the design. He thought it was suited to Stanford, whatever that thought had meant to his eighteen-year-old brain.

Design, construction and art push away his thoughts of calling anyone at all. He runs his fingers over the bedspread and then, with his right index finger, his hand begins to trace out a set of shapes. He traces it five, six times without knowing what it is he doodles with his finger as a stylus. He can keep his nail on the fabric and only pick it up once and put it back down once to get the entire design down. He cranes his neck up and over to his right to try and watch what it is his body is doing without conscious effort on his part, but the only light that comes from the open window is weak, a street lamp down the road from his cul-de-sac.

If only he had a pen and some paper, he could get the doodle down and make sense of it when he was less inebriated. But his body is leaden, his foot tingling with promises of elevated pain, because the alcohol and OxyContin are wearing off. He pushes his face into the worn bedspread and lets his finger drawn lines on the old cotton without giving it further attention.

"I'll remember to draw it in the morning," he speaks to the room. And then he's in the void of sleep, waking with a start only once when a dream takes him to a possible world, an alternate reality where he lost both feet to the serrated teeth of a monstrous fish and upon escape from it, he lay with his belly soft against the earth. His thick, near-black blood seeped into the dirt, helping the powers of spring in their task of thawing the clay and sand, letting the earth take away his life.

LATE WINTER, 1992

24   PEACH

When her foster parents hand her a Cabbage Patch doll with sandy blond hair and green eyes, they tell her they had it made special for Peach and she can name the doll Peach or any other name she'd like. They tell her the doll was made to look just like their new ward, to welcome her into their home.

Peach doesn't point out the one problem with the soft-bodied doll: Peach's eyes are hazel, not green. But she sleeps with the doll at night, aware at nine years of age, she should be breaking the habit of liking dolls, not getting new ones. But the house is a new place, the woman smells of chicken soup no matter what she eats and the man sets out to work an hour ahead of schedule so he can bike alongside all the cars on the road instead of drive alongside them. This house is nothing like the home from which she was just ripped away. That house was a home. This house is a house. But the doll is comforting and she takes the people at their word, that they got the doll especially for her.

She goes to a new school, eats at a new dining table. This one is oak. She sleeps in a double bed, not a twin bed, and has her own room this time. She does her best not to think of the Barrows or her foster brothers and sister, the people who'd been with her in the house turned into her home. Six weeks have passed since she was removed from there, deposited here. And the doll remains at her side while she learns to live in this house. Peach looks into the flat, painted eyes of the doll and decides maybe she does have green eyes. This man and this woman have given her a doll that is supposed to be just like her. And if they say she has green eyes, she must have green eyes. So she stares into mirrors, turns her head toward light, away from light, and decides yes, her eyes indeed are green.

And when she has truly convinced herself her eyes are green and not hazel, she finally names the doll Peach. This Peach has soft, yellow yarn for hair and a cherubic face. The doll's dress is made of blue, clingy fabric that gets snagged on the Velcro closure of Peach's backpack. She gets by in the house, with this set of man and woman, by carrying around a version of herself.

Until she hears the man and the woman speaking one afternoon while she does her math homework at the island in their kitchen. They're talking about finances in the other room and Peach only catches some of what they say. She doesn't make a point to listen intently. She learned long ago the trick to staying in foster homes longer than a few weeks was to be as complacent and silent as possible.

But then the woman says something about Peach and income. And then the little Peach, the fake Peach made of plastic and a soft, cotton body is brought up. It turns out that the doll was not bought just for her. It was used, a hand-me-down from the last girl who was in the house.

Peach goes to her room and shuts the door. The doll is on the bed and she scoops it up in her arms and cradles it close to her neck. The plastic is impregnated with the smell of baby powder and smooth to the touch. She looks into fake Peach's eyes and frowns.

Peach knew her eyes were hazel, not green. But she had been told otherwise, told what she should be, and she did her best to be it because "being it," whatever people wanted her to be, was the key to survival in the foster system. She pulls the pencil she was using for her long division out of her pocket and throws the doll down on the bed. Over and over, she plunges the pencil through the green eyes of the doll whom Peach feels has more identity than her. The doll never tries to be anything but a doll. A doll with green eyes. The pencil tip breaks, a sharp point of graphite sails off into the carpet of the room, lost.

FALL,
1990

25   RILEY

He plays a Native American, a member of the Wampanoag tribe, in a short kindergarten skit put on for students and their parents right before Thanksgiving break. The entire play lasts fifteen minutes. One of the ears of corn gets distracted by a tune only she can hear and breaks into a spastic, jerky dance while Riley delivers his line. He stays stoic—as he imagines all Native Americans are from what he's seen on television—and puts his hand on his chest.

"I bring eel to eat," he says and then he bows, a touch all his own.

And his parents cannot get the costume of the paper bag headdress and the apron made of scrap suede from his mother's sewing stash off of his body. He insists on staying a Native American and his parents joke that he's "gone native," turning their faces away to laugh when he hollers out battle cries and whips an imaginary horse around their living room settee.

The Alberstons bag goes soft and rips from continual wear.

The suede is stained with his sweat and lunchtime sandwiches of peanut butter and raspberry jelly. When he speaks to adults, he's polite and sparse with his words. But when he plays with his friends, those children he's identified as part of his tribe, he's untamable, free of pretention. Riley decides he should stay a Native American forever.

His interest in eel as a food plagues him and thus his parents, and at his constant prodding, they finally look into getting him some eel to eat. Except Boise, Idaho is not near an ocean and does not have a significant Japanese population. There is nowhere to find eel as food and so they compromise with Riley and take him to a pet store with an extensive aquarium section.

There he presses his nose to rectangular containers full of saltwater and spies the electric blue eyes of a monster. The eel has an elongated face and a strong underbite decorated with needle-like teeth. Its mouth gapes open and Riley opens his in response. He locks eyes with the fish that looks like a snake, held captive by its strange presence. His parents pry him away and he cries on the ride home, ripping his headdress from his hair as white as beach sand, tossing it to the floor mat at his feet.

His mother turns around and smiles at her son, her hands grasping the side of the passenger seat. Her wavy hair billows around the headrest and there is a smear of purple lipstick on her upper teeth.

"I see you're done being a native?" she asks and then pats him on the leg. "That's good, Riley. You're not a real Native American anyway. All your ancestors came from Europe a long time ago. You don't need an excuse to be a wild little boy. Europeans have been wild enough through the ages."

When he hears this from his mother, he stops his crying about the eel and desperately tries to reach down to the torn and crumpled brown bag at his feet, lines of crayon approximating feathers and beads at the rim of the cap. But his seatbelt restrains him, his arms too short to get back the costume and put it on his head. He's helpless, unable to go native again and sits back, feels the anger necessary for a resplendent tantrum building in his head and gut and finally screams and weeps because he is nothing more than a plain, white boy.

SATURDAY, THE 28TH OF MARCH, 2015

26 PEACH

She wears a dress that dips in a wide V down the front of her chest. The deep burgundy color complements her skin tone, making her white flesh luminescent in the candlelight. The dress had been too long even for her long legs, so she had to hem the bottom. The stitches were crooked and if one looked closely, it was easy to see the slinky fabric was bunched and bulbous because of the poorly done sewing. But Peach was counting, yet again, on people's inability to notice details. So many of her choices were riding on that one assumption alone. Most people were so inattentive, so enraptured with themselves, she was convinced she could commit murder here, in this fine Italian restaurant, and someone would order another glass of Prosecco.

Linx picks at a sprig of rosemary alive and thriving in a small pot in the center of their table. He rubs one of the dark green needles and then brings his hand up to Peach's nose.

"Smell that. That's what all of Tuscany must smell like," he says and then pours himself a glass of water from a carafe stacked with ice and lemon.

Peach pulls up on her dress. The cut was unusual for her to wear. She didn't usually enjoy showing that much breast, and as soon as she got to the restaurant and noted how Linx was staring at her chest, she regretted her choice in attire. She hadn't put the outfit on for him. It was for her. A celebratory gesture, something suggested to her when she spoke the other night with the stars. Peach had to treat herself right during her time of transformation.

"The meat is a bit dry. It should just fall off the bone. But the tomatoes are vibrant," she says and pushes the lamb osso buco around on her plate. She doesn't particularly enjoy eating lamb, but she had to have it when she saw it on the menu. She thinks of a paper placemat she read at a Chinese restaurant in late January. 2015 is the Year of the Sheep.

"You look nice," Linx says and takes a swig of water. "Beautiful, I mean. Not nice. Nice is too plain. Radiant? I like radiant. Wait, that's a word, right?"

She smiles at his question and nods at him and then at her dish. Linx's first generation American status meant he struggled with vocabulary on occasion. He was better off than his mother, a tiny Thai woman, petite even by her own country's standards, who spoke nearly all her sentences in a mishmash of English and tonal Thai.

Sawing a piece of meat from the hollow bone in the middle of her dish, Peach brings the flesh up to her tongue and bites down mindfully. It tastes like springtime.

"Have you ever seen how rams will just run at one another, the males, that is, and butt one another so hard with their horns they become dazed and just stagger around for a moment? And then they do it again. Why do you think they do it?" Peach poses the question to her dinner mate and cleans a bit of the osso buco sauce up with a slice of crusty bread.

Linx twirls his pappardelle around on his plate. A piece of

wilted spinach clings to his fork. "Mating. They're fighting over the woman sheep, Peach."

"Ewes," she corrects him, envisioning a bizarre creature with the head of Angelina Jolie and the thick, black body of an unshorn sheep. Peach was expecting Linx to give her that answer. Something rote and textbook. Linx had the tendency to avoid deep consideration of questions when he could pop off a basic answer and get back to more pleasant conversation. But she felt the rams must *like* the pain. She imagines how it must feel to crush bone on bone, to smash your head into another person's head and come out victorious in whatever it is you're fighting for.

She supposes both humans and sheep do battle in the same way. With their heads. One powered with wit, the other, with hormones. In some human cases, with both wit and hormones, or neither.

"Right," she says, "but there are always enough ewes to go around. I think, in the end, the rams are fighting more for themselves and less for the flock of sheep."

Linx puts down his utensil and takes up rubbing the plant again. He opens his mouth to speak but Peach beats him to it.

"I guess the question is, do you make the decision to fight or not fight? Choice. That's what makes up the plot of our lives. To ram skulls or not? Even if it kills you."

Linx releases the plant and waves down the waiter. A man in black pants and a white button down arrives at the side of the table and Linx orders a panna cotta with black cherry sauce for them to split.

"You're radiant," he tells Peach, over-enunciating the word, "but you can be confusing. So, you want to make some life changes?"

"You've known me for years," she replies. "I need to change. I need a big change."

What he replies with catches her off-guard. She coughs on a

piece of salty crust as it travels down her throat.

"I like you as you are. But if you want change, then be my partner, my girlfriend. Officially. That would be a change. We'd be out of the limbo we're currently in. I could actually sleep over."

"Linx," she starts but doesn't get a chance to explain away her inability to commit with some small falsehood. Linx holds up a hand for her to stop.

"I know. Not now. Not yet. I'm not the change you're looking for, right? Even if I'm nothing like Adam."

The name makes Peach put down her fork and drop her chin.

She looks down at the cut of meat left on her plate. Some delicate, fresh baby was butchered for her meal. And she's taking the lamb's energy and using it to power discussions about a relationship she doesn't wish to have with her best friend. The lamb could have lived its life on a hillock of deep green pasture instead. But it was now a part of her meal, in this dish and dancing with the bile in her stomach at this very moment.

"Do you know," she starts, noticing the waiter making his way through the crowded dining room with their dessert, "that the recipe I'm eating is traditionally made with veal? But it can be made with any sort of meat. Because what died in order to make something phenomenal isn't important. It's the *cut* of the meat that is."

Peach lifts her hand and pokes a finger straight though a marrow-less section of bone. Linx barely looks at her, his mind on his inability to lock down his heart's desire.

"Osso buco means 'bone hole.'" She brings the bone up, held by her index finger. A trickle of juice and sauce smelling of wine and thyme runs down her wrist. "This is what I feel like sometimes, Linx. Hollow bones. And if you can't use them to fly, you just feel like you're made of emptiness."

Linx reaches over and presses the bone and her hand back

down to the plate. The waiter lifts an eyebrow at Peach as he sets the white custard on the table and backs away. She eyes the cherry sauce and notes that it looks like coagulated blood. Yet it gives off a scent of deep, summertime sweetness.

"Then fill yourself up," Linx says.

"I'm trying," Peach replies.

MONDAY, THE 30TH OF MARCH, 2015

27   RILEY

It's strange not to head into work on a Monday morning.
Riley tosses around in bed until his room is completely swamped
with light from the midmorning sun. He normally would be at
work by now, putting an hour or two of sweat into sanding down
sharp edges on grating to place on machines meant for separating
the gold out of worthless soil.

Now, he had nothing to keep him occupied. Except his foot.
And his conquest of Nell. He hadn't forgotten what he'd sworn
to do last Friday night. The more he thought about it, the more
intensely he wanted her. Claiming her would be a victory for
Riley. A chest pounding, testosterone-fueled self-esteem boost.
And he thought if he could name it what it was, it was okay to
want it.

He wanted to feel like a whole, American man again. After
all he'd been through in the past few years. And now, after the
anvil, he wanted it even more.

Nell would be a means to his selfish end.

His crutches carry him down the stairs to his kitchen where his cell phone is plugged in, battery charging since last night. He pulls the cord out of the phone and eyes the screen. He's had three calls, all from Double Al, no voicemails. He smiles, thinks of all the blue-collar assholes who he works with, *worked* with, missing their whipping boy on Monday morning. Because no matter how hard he strove to learn the job and fit in, he was always a pretty boy lawyer to them. And no loss of limbs would likely give him more credibility. It might actually take the small respect they had for his abilities completely away.

He taps Double Al's name when he calls it up on the phone screen and after two rings the man picks up.

"Son," he says for a greeting, "how's the foot?"

"I'm sure the toes will grow back in no time. That's how it works right? I failed basic anatomy and biology a few times."

Double Al doesn't humor him with a laugh. His voice is strong, true.

"I've been calling because I've been thinking about what happened to you last week. I haven't been sleeping much. I keep thinking about doing a safety check on all the shop tools. And for some reason I think it needs to be done at 3am."

"Accidents," Riley says and then ventures a guess at what's really bothering Double Al. "I'm not suing you. If that's what you're worried about."

The line goes quiet for a moment and then Double Al speaks, a hint of incredulous defensiveness in his voice. "No. I'm not worried about that at all. I'm actually worried about you, son. I want you to come back to work."

"I just lost the toes a week ago. I wouldn't be of any use to the work soccer team." Riley laughs at his own joke and tucks the phone tight against his ear and his shoulder. He hobbles his way over to the refrigerator and pulls out a loaf of wheat bread and sets it next to his toaster.

"I don't mean today," Double Al replies, all business. "But I do mean for you to come back. In whatever capacity you choose."

Riley smiles and drops a piece of bread in the toaster. He knows Double Al doesn't expect him to be capable of manual labor immediately after the accident. He'll probably want to tuck him away in an office somewhere, making cold calls to recreational miners and sending emails to gold websites to garner cross promotion of products.

He starts to speak but Double Al cuts him off.

"Don't answer me now. Just know that I'll demand you back eventually. I want you to rest up and heal. And when you're up for getting out I'm going to take you to dinner and I'll convince you to come back. By my word, I will."

"Okay," Riley says, nearly losing his grip on the phone between his cheek and shoulder. "I'll let you woo me when I can look my best."

"No joke," his boss pushes and then hangs up without a mention of farewell.

Riley puts the phone down and watches as the metal coils in the toaster glow cherry red. The bread turns from brown to black as he stares into the appliance. He thinks it's strange one can watch something transform, but not be able to point out when the change actually occurs. When the bread moves from soft to hard, light to dark.

On Riley's refrigerator is the drawing Tate sent him on his last birthday. He looks it over again, noting the careful attention the young boy had put into scribbling chartreuse on the paper to approximate grass under the feet of five and six-legged bovines. The large, human-sized golden eagle is where the kid must have put in the hours. Brown feathers are outlined in black marker and the bird's eyes stare out of the picture, circles of gold glitter glue ringing nearly perfect dots of black. He wonders what Tate does now, at his home in Weiser, Idaho with Riley's ex-girlfriend, Kristin. He wonders if Tate does more drawings, sends them out to other men having birthdays, men who could also potentially be Tate's biological father.

His finger is moving again like it did the night he passed out in his guest room, tracing the same pattern over and over on the countertop as he waits for his toast. When it pops free of the toaster, Riley picks back up his phone and thumbs through his contacts until he finds one labeled *Crucible*. He hits the send button and decides if he should dress his toast in butter or Nutella.

TUESDAY, THE 31ST OF MARCH, 2015

28 PEACH

Peach wonders if creepers like their sex at the beginning of the week. Though it's a Tuesday, Blaze Lounge is alive with men looking for succor or company in the shadow of tan, cosmetically-enhanced strippers.

She instantly regrets wearing the mauve lambswool sweater and bringing in a fleece jacket tucked under her arm. While the air is still chill outside, inside the strip club the atmosphere is stuffy and hot and smells of sweat and drugstore cologne. She makes her way through the large front room with the stage, weaving around tables to the back of the room. The eyes of the clientele rake across her body as she moves. As far as she can tell, she's the only female in the place who isn't dressed in pasties and a thong, gyrating to bad music on stage or tending bar.

She claims a small table in the darkest corner of the place and takes a seat. The legs of the table are uneven and the wobble makes her feel antsy. She swipes a small stack of drink coasters off a neighboring table and tucks them under the short leg. Then she tries to calm herself. She takes deep breaths. Occasionally one of the men glances back her way, but she doesn't make eye contact with any of them. She keeps her face forward, focuses on one dancer who does a shabby job dancing in cowboy boots and a small cowboy hat made of floppy leather, a black string running under her chin, keeping it on her head. Her costume is fringed suede concealing all the parts of her form Idaho law says she can't show to the public. Peach can't tell what color the dark leather is in the low light of the room, but the pieces of choppy fabric sway when she dips, spins, shakes. Peach imagines the woman having to ride a Palomino, cook sliced potatoes over a campfire, and rustle cattle all while donning those skimpy bits of cowhide.

The hair of the stripper peeks out from under the cowboy hat. It's the kind of purple red that only comes from a tube of chemicals and the front of her hair hangs in long panels at the sides of her face, growing shorter toward the back of her head. It transitions to neatly shorn, shorter than the hair of most traditionally-minded men, when it reaches the spot where neck meets skull.

A waitress comes to Peach's table, her body's curves hugged by a tight satin jumpsuit.

"Can I get you something, honey?"

"Just water," Peach says and then remembers her manners before the woman walks away. "For now. Thank you."

The truth is Peach won't order alcohol. She's never gotten past the way all booze, upon hitting her tongue, makes her think of the rubbing alcohol that had been blotted on her knees. The time both of them were pulpy, bloody, strips of skin hanging off her kneecaps and bits of broken shale rock and sand embedded in the wounds. That zippy smell of isopropyl alcohol that shot through her nose to her mouth would always be associated with fear and confusion and the shattering of morals.

And she hates the way it dulls her senses.

The stripper with the fake red hair and large, buoyant breasts continues her shuffle across the stage. A man stands and wanders to the edge of the runway. His mouth is turned up in a sneer as he tucks a solitary dollar into the waist of her panties.

"Baby."

Peach hears another man's voice but doesn't realize he's talking to her until he takes a seat at her table. He's a short man, middling years, with a large gut that hangs over his belt and tight Wranglers. She wonders if Tuesday night is a theme night, Rodeo or Cowboy, and she didn't get the memo.

She doesn't respond to him, even when he sits. She crosses her arms in front of her body, looks to the entrance, the way out.

"I'm not hitting on you, blondie. I'm the owner." The man says this with his chin lifted, his eyes wide.

Peach lets her down her guard a bit. While she doesn't want attention from the owner, at least it's not a member of a bachelor party or a drunken lout certain his chances of nailing her are high.

"Okay," she says. "Hello."

"You look a bit like my mother, when she was young," he says and Peach nods her head in acknowledgement.

The owner of Blaze Lounge talks directly to her breasts, not even trying to hide where his gaze is locked. Peach considers he's probably used to looking at chests, in a professional and salacious manner, all day long. Why should her chest be any different?

"You want a job?" he asks.

"What?" Peach stutters a bit. "No, thank you."

"Well you should think on it, on account of those big titties you have," he says, eyes never leaving the product he covets. "You'd make good money here."

Peach shifts a bit in her seat, brings her arms up higher to cover more of her body from his heavy stare.

"No, not interested," she repeats and tries to focus on the stripper.

"Right," the man laughs and pushes his belly out as he rocks around on his buttocks. The chair scrapes on the floor, makes a sound like a kettle of water at full boil.

"Just thought I'd ask. You're in here so much, I figured you wanted something. I see you a few times a week. Though I don't mind if you just wanna watch. You're allowed to be a regular, now. Welcome. Feel free to rub one out in the pisser."

Peach smirks, anxious he'll begin to study her face after his assessment of her breasts. She puts up a hand, leans on her palm, turns away her chin. The man keeps his place next to her, attention turned to the stage, eyes on the stripper's body draped in leather. His shin thwacks against the leg of the table she just stabilized and when the redheaded stripper ends her dance, he puts two short fingers in his mouth and salutes her with a piercing whistle.

29   RILEY

"I can't believe you won't give me a ride," Riley yells into the phone. He's sure a speck of saliva has landed on his screen but he's too annoyed to wipe it off on his shirt.

"It's a Tuesday. And it's late afternoon. I'm still at work, Rye. I have a meeting at six tonight. There's no way I can take you to the strip club today. Get over it." Walker's voice is tight and clipped.

Riley holds the phone away from his mouth and hits the speaker button. "I need to get going on this thing with the stripper, Walker. It's what I'm doing right now. I've got to get to work on bagging her. And I can't really do that from my house, now can I?"

"It was a good thing you never had to argue a case in court. I'm going to hang up on you. Seriously."

Riley closes his eyes and grits his teeth. He only wants one thing to go his way. And he believes this one thing is Nell. Whether Walker helps him is his choice. But he won't beg his friend.

"Fine. Go to your boring meeting. I'm going to lie down and watch tennis or something."

He can hear the way Walker's voice lightens. "Good choice. Stay off your feet so you can heal, brother. I'll check up with you later."

But when Riley tosses his phone on the couch, he doesn't let his body go with it. He doesn't want to rest. He's restless.

He makes his way sans crutches to a storage closet near the door to his garage. He uses his hands against the plastered walls to hop his way there and pulls a small plastic tote down from a shelf inside the closet. He makes sure his feet are out of the way and then he lets the bin drop to the floor instead of gently placing it down. Riley steadies himself with one arm on his taupe-colored wall and flips the lid off with his other hand.

The bin is full of old track trophies, yearbooks from high school, pictures paper-clipped together in small stacks. He rummages around until he produces a well-used footbag, actual Hacky Sack brand. It's red, yellow and green, the colors he associates with Rastafarians, but scuffed with dirt and its pigmentation muted from use and years. The weaving is hemp and the inside is full of little beans. It gives a bit in his clenched fist.

He leaves the tote open, memorabilia scattered around on the floor and jumps his way to his living room and the couch where he tossed his phone. He looks at his abandoned crutches pitched against his entertainment center and can't stand the thought of watching tennis players volley and sprint around a court while he's bereft of half his toes. He hops over to his coat closet and pulls a right running shoe and a left snow boot out from a shoe rack.

Sitting on his couch, he squishes the hard footbag in his hands, feels the weight of the old toy he used to kick around with his friends during lulls at track meets. It might be too heavy for the purpose he has in mind, but he's anxious to see if it will work.

Tucking the bag down into the toe of the snow boot, he maneuvers the beans around until it's flush against the boot's edge. He puts the running shoe on his right foot, ties up the laces. Then he puts his left foot, freshly bandaged with new gauze, into the snow boot.

He lucks out. His wound doesn't completely ram into the bag, but it does touch at all the points where his toes used to be. He grimaces in pain but drops the weight of his heel in the boot anyway. He screams out, balls his fists and smacks the cushions of the couch.

Riley stands then, again without his crutches, and steps only on the heel of his left foot to get to his front door. Lightning shots of agony race up his body, but he refuses to take off the boot and tend to his injury. The afternoon greets him; the sky is overcast and the wind smells of impending rain.

He makes it to the end of his driveway at a steady gimp, putting most of his weight on his right foot and skipping a little when his left needs to touch the ground.

There, at the street gutter clogged with patches of last fall's leaves, Riley steps off onto the street and starts to run.

And five steps later, he's falling, his movements unsustainable, his right foot cramping, his left pulsating with hurt. He catches himself with his palms, swearing as he scuffs his hands on the rough landing. He heaves in deep breaths on all four limbs, his back arching like a stretching housecat.

Riley watches a pill bug with its gray armor traverse the small bumps in the asphalt. A tear escapes one of his eyes and splashes down next to the insect. The impact of the teardrop on the road must be like the cascade of an unexpected waterfall to the creature. The shock causes the bug to curl up its exoskeleton into a tight ball. Riley blows on the small being hidden in its casing. It spins away, until Riley can't make it out against the light black of the pavement.

He's not ashamed to admit he enjoys, on occasion, taking out his frustrations on things smaller and weaker than himself. He feels it is part of his biological programming, some bit of a gene which firmly establishes him as a man. And as a man, others are sometimes forced to reckon with his superiority.

"I win," he sobs, crawling on all fours back to his driveway.

"I fucking win."

30 PEACH

The stripper is missing from the stage for awhile and Peach scans the room to try and figure out where she went. Then she catches sight of the woman in her silly Western garb as she moves out a pneumatic-hinged emergency exit. Peach stands and considers going out the same door after her, but thinks it might look weird to follow one of the dancers. She doesn't want to be noticed anymore than she's already been. The owner of Blaze Lounge had retreated from her table once Peach had stopped answering his questions and she sees him now, at the bar, a plastic basket of barbeque wings in his grasp.

She leaves out the main entrance and wanders around the outside of the building, worried the woman will have disappeared out of her vicinity and her life. The neon flames on the top of the club aren't lit yet and commuters rush by on the busy thoroughfare running next to the lounge. Peach turns a corner and sees the dancer leaning against a white concrete wall. She decides she can't possibly talk to the woman and turns to move away. But the dancer sees her and yells out.

"You're the only girl in there," she says and Peach turns back around. "I mean, not working. I like women. They smell nicer and don't touch during lap dances."

Peach clears her throat and takes shuffling steps toward the dancer. She transfers her fleece jacket from hand to hand and stops a few feet away from the stripper. The woman is smoking a peach-flavored Prime Time. Peach can smell the sweetness of her namesake in the lit cigarillo.

The stripper is shivering in her skimpy outfit. Peach looks at her fleece jacket and holds it out to the woman. "You cold?"

"Thanks," the dancer says. She holds the cigarillo in her mouth and reaches out for the jacket. She swings it over her shoulders, leaving her arms free to rub at her bare thighs.

"So are you a lesbian or are you wanting to dance?"

Peach looks at the woman's cowboy boots. They're the antithesis of real Western boots. These have platform heels.

"I don't dance well," Peach responds.

"So you like girls?"

She doesn't answer instantly and the stripper moves away from the subject, astute enough to see Peach squirm. Her fingers dart upwards to pull the cigarillo from her lips. "I dance to sleep more than anything else."

"How's that?"

"I'm an insomniac," the stripper says. "For some reason, the dancing helps me sleep at night. Might be the exercise. I guess I could just go to the gym, but I wouldn't get paid there."

She snickers at her own joke and Peach laughs along for a moment before growing quiet again. Peach studies the woman's face and her body with subtle gazes. She can't believe she's standing next to her. It's an unreal moment for Peach and she feels a tingling throughout her entire body, but especially in the depths of her pelvis.

The metal side door swings open and Peach has to move to

escape from being hit by its weight. A big man in a leather jacket emerges, a frown on his face.

He doesn't notice Peach at first, just narrows his focus solely on the stripper. He looks around the area where they all stand, like he's on alert for wild dogs or enemy combatants.

"Didn't see you leave, love," he quips.

"Just out for a smoke" she says to him but smiles at Peach. Peach smiles back and cannot believe she's smiling at *her*.

It's then the man notices Peach. She's thrown by his size. The backs of his hands are decorated with raised veins the size of her pinkie fingers. His ears, pierced through with gold rings, are double the size of her own.

He nods at her and Peach first thinks it's in greeting, but then realizes it's to point her out to the dancer.

"Who's the enchantress?"

Peach can't contain her smile when she hears what he's called her. A tickle starts at the base of her spine and dallies around her lower back until she has to rub it away with an open palm. All of her body is at attention.

"I'm Peach," she says and delivers her rehearsed line. "Just doing research."

"I'm Sev," he responds and takes the cigarillo from the stripper and pulls out the last drags of smoke it holds. "And this is my girl, Nell."

Peach almost says, *I know*. The words get out of her before she can stop them, but she's able to catch her voice mid-breath and spin it into something absurd.

"Idaho," Peach gets out. "I mean, welcome to Idaho, Sev."

The man tosses the spent tobacco to the ground and shakes his head.

"Strange," he says and pulls open the side door. Nell slips in before him and gives a little wave to Peach before adjusting the leather string running along her ribcage. He motions for Peach to come back in but she doesn't move, watching her fleece jacket leave, spread across the shoulders of the woman she dreams of and has thought about for so long.

Before the man goes back inside, he looks at Peach and purses his lips. "Isn't that what the main characters in the Chinese fairytale, *Journey to the West*, are looking for? The Monkey King wants it, right?"

"What's that? I'm not a literature buff. I stick to science fiction," she answers.

"A peach," he says, "to give him immortality. I think it was a peach."

She shrugs her shoulders and walks away from the hulking man. Nell. Nell Hyde. She considers it a good stage name. As she moves back to her Honda, away from the temptations sheltered in Blaze Lounge, she thinks of quests for unobtainable things, thinks of what people are willing to do for the rarest of grails.

WEDNESDAY, THE 1ST OF APRIL, 2015

31 RILEY

Though his mailbox is at the end of his driveway, Riley
speculates his regular mailman must have seen him try to run the
other day and fall on the street outside of his house. Because
today, his mail has been tucked neatly under the sage coir
welcome mat outside of his front door.

The morning is colder than usual. A frost hit the night
before; he can see the apricot blossoms on his neighbor's tree did
not survive the freeze. He rubs his arms and balances on his right
foot, hinges at the waist and goes down in a makeshift yoga pose
to pluck up his mail.

Riley nearly stumbles on the door threshold back into his
open foyer. He hops to the living room and lowers himself down
on his brown leather couch. He focuses on controlling his
descent, regaining some physical composure one day at a time.
His left foot fared poorly from his attempted run the day before.
The use of the footbag for more stability in the snow boot had
caused too much pressure on the wound. He'd had to peel the

gauze from the tines of the stitches, working at each piece of cotton gently to keep from pulling at the healing skin.

He shuffles the mail in his hands. There's a flyer for a local pizza place and two offers for credit cards. And at the bottom of the pile is a card.

He doesn't need to look at the writing to know it's from the same sender as the card he opened in the hospital. The feel of dried wax on the underside of the envelope tells him through his fingertips. He tosses aside the other mail and breathes out hard.

The impress of the wax is similar to the seal on the first card, but this oval is slightly bigger and he guesses that whatever is being pushed into the wax is something organic, a bit asymmetrical. His name and address are spelled out in the same tilted, curly writing.

Like last time, he rips the side off of the envelope to preserve the wax seal. The content is a card; the cover displays a photograph of a meadow of wildflowers in pinks and white with a placid lake in the middle distance.

It had been a blank card inside, its message added by hand. Riley reads this card out loud:

You're healthy, wealthy and wise! People adore you because of your successful career and your giving spirit. Luck follows you wherever you go. Best yet, you have a family that loves you and considers you top priority!

April Fool!

Life's Fool!

Love,

Hamal

Riley clenches the envelope in his hand, wadding it into a tight ball of wrinkles. Some of the maroon wax chips off the seal and drops to his jeans. He doesn't know why this stranger insists on sending him cards, but this note is harsher than the other, more obscure communication. He wonders if it's a cruel joke being played on him by his coworkers at High Desert Trommel.

His face drops, his eyes widen and his stomach does a flip. It takes a moment for Riley to realize what's going on with his body. But then his heart catches up to his mind and he admits it. His feelings are hurt.

He shuts the card and stares at the photograph plastered on the front. It's a scene of beginning, of springtime and awakenings. But all he can focus on is the dreary lake in the distance. The surface of the water is staid and Riley imagines he stands at the pond's edge, taking in an expanse of stagnation. To Riley, the shore smells sharply of dried out algae and the piquant stink of fish.

32   PEACH

There's no use in Peach trying to focus on her client reports. Though it's only midmorning, she's coming down from her experience yesterday with Nell. She almost can't believe she was bold enough to talk to the stripper and even let her wear her coat. It's then that she realizes she never got the fleece jacket back from her. She imagines it smells like stale tobacco with a hint of artificial peach.

She pulls a small Moleskine notebook from her white and tan purse tucked under her desk. She touches the soft binding. It's a deep teal color and has an elastic band to keep the pages together and free from wrinkles. She doesn't flip it open. Instead she places it on her desk and puts her cheek down on it, resting her head and shutting her eyes.

The sensation of the firm binding touching her skin and the smell of the pages reminds her of the Bible she used to lay her face on during Sunday Mass. Though she only went to St. Mary's briefly during her childhood and rarely when she was with Adam, she could remember how the weight and shape of the Bible would push back against her cheekbone. She'd get askance glares from other parishioners but she always told herself putting your face, the mask you present to the world, on the Bible, was like baring yourself to God.

This notebook is thinner and squatter, but the contents of the pages are no less important to Peach's life and future goals.

Sheep wander into Peach's mind. She heard somewhere that of all the animals mentioned in the Bible, sheep are written about the most. She can believe it. The Jews were shepherds. Peach feels like a shepherd, always tending her charges, anxious to control their lives. A good shepherd will lay down her life for the flock. And all the shepherd asks for in exchange is the very same. Some sheep might provide wool. Others milk. Others meat. But they all have their uses to the shepherd. Otherwise, what purpose do they serve for the shepherd's life?

Peach thinks about the Bible study classes made mandatory while she lived with one foster couple with the last name of Dorset. Then she calls to mind the yellow cake Adam would insist on making each Easter they were together. It was baked in a metal form pan and when turned out on wax paper, a lamb, legs tucked under its body, would be ready for decoration. They never ate the lamb, choosing to let the white frosting and sprigs of grass wrought with sugary gel dry out and harden to an inedible shell.

But the classes, she remembers, make her realize now that sheep got a lot of people killed in the Bible. Abel, the first shepherd, felt a murderous blow from his brother Cain. And Isaac or Ishmael—his name debatable amongst the religious groups following Yahweh—was nearly dispatched on the whim of the Old Testament God. Peach whispers to her office the Bible passage she memorized long ago.

"Abraham looked up and there in a thicket he saw a ram caught by its horns. He went over and took the ram and

120

sacrificed it as a burnt offering instead of his son."

She knows there is a word for the sacrifice of a ram: criobolium. Except in her mind this term doesn't apply to sacrifices made to the god Yahweh. It refers to the act of spilling sheep's blood in devotion to other gods, many of them lost to modern man.

Peach imagines how Abraham's hands must have tussled with the strong, ribbed prongs of the ram. He surely came away bloodied from the work. She feels this is only right; when a blood offering is made, your own blood is spilt as well.

The ram, the blood, the fire. Three important things. It's a good story. Simple, but engaging. And the son makes it out alive in the end. Whether it was Isaac or Ishmael up for slaughter doesn't matter much. Abraham was just being a good shepherd. He was just asking for sacrifice.

FRIDAY,
THE 3RD OF APRIL,
2015

33   RILEY

The bottle of Jameson is empty, the cap spinning between Riley's fingers. Homebound and alone, he can do little more than stew in thoughts of past mistakes and future goals. He can see Nell dancing in front of him wearing a purple bikini. Her skin has a shimmer to it, flecks of glitter reflecting the blue and pink accent lights which line the ceiling over the place she writhes and gyrates. She's a beacon, a flickering flame Riley looks to capture and turn into a raging fire.

He licks the rim of the whiskey bottle. The stripper isn't even that pretty. He's not really into redheads and fake boobs and he wonders what she looks like in direct sunlight, in khakis and a modest top, sans makeup. Riley would find her unremarkable, her beauty too dependent on the scalpel and low-lighting and his frequent inebriation.

But it isn't her looks ultimately keeping her at the forefront of his brain. It's her low social status which attracts him. Because as down as Riley feels, he figures he's not as bad off as a woman having to sell the movements of her body for cash. If he claims Nell in bed, he reasserts his primacy, status and worth in life. Getting Nell on her back and under him is the first step to Riley reestablishing himself as a winner.

"I had a little accident," Riley says to the empty bottle. He's practicing for when he has to tell the two people he chose not to call the other night about his missing toes. "And let's just say I won't be wearing peep toe pumps anytime soon. Shit, how the hell do I know what a peep toe is anyway?"

Walker comes in the front door. Riley decided it would be best to pre-funk before going out on the town with his friend. Walker's wearing a fuchsia dress shirt and trousers that hug his muscular body. His friend had given up on asking Riley to go to the gym with him; Riley hated lifting though Walker was addicted to it. Riley only ever wanted to run. Walker's face is newly tanned and his brown hair is carefully styled, a sweeping part gelled over his left eye. He takes a look at Riley on the leather couch and shakes his head.

"I thought you were on the phone, Rye. But you're just talking to yourself."

"I am a man of talents. And this whiskey bottle can attest to that," Riley says and hands the bottle to Walker, holding it tight at the long neck.

"I'll trade you," Walker says, takes the glass bottle and exchanges it for a single piece of mail. "It's got a tread mark on it from my shoe. But that's what happens when mailmen leave letters where people walk."

Riley's eyes get bigger and he knows it's another piece of mail from the stranger before seeing a bit of writing or a wax seal. "Seriously? Another one."

"More mail? Yep, I get it at my house six times a week, too," Walker says and plops down on a La-Z-Boy recliner in the corner of the room. It was one of the pieces of furniture Riley kept after cleaning out his parents' house. After the crash.

124

"Nah," Riley says and runs his hands over the familiar writing and the dark, blobby wax. "This is different."

He pries open the side of the tan envelope and produces the third card from the mysterious sender. It has a picture of a white daylily on the front and the word *Rejoice* is typed in pink font. The message inside is printed in black ink: *May the risen Lord cleanse you of all your sins this Easter. Blessings for a year of new beginnings and resurrected hope.*

And under this message is the same slanted printing he's seen on the other two cards. This message is less cryptic and more commanding:

Brunch is so gauche and bourgeois. These days, everyone is having breakfast at a decent hour. How about you have an Easter breakfast downtown this Sunday? Try a restaurant in the Basque block, but don't show up too late. If you do, you'll regret it!

Love,

Hamal

Riley keeps his eyes on the card but motions to Walker to stand up. "Go into the kitchen and get the two cards next to my phone charger."

His friend doesn't protest. Walker slips off the chair and retrieves the first two cards. Riley hands him the one he's just opened. Walker reads them all, pokes at the wax seals and rubs his eyes. "Who the hell is Hamal?"

"No idea," Riley says and puts out his hand for the messages. "That card you brought to the hospital was the first one. Then the second came on April Fool's Day. And this one came today. I feel so loved."

"I'd take this shit seriously, Rye. This person sounds like a nutcase. Have you reported it?"

Riley laughs and sets the cards down on a glass coffee table with brass legs. "Report it? What, like tell the mailman and have him defend my honor? I'm guessing some of the guys I work with are messing with me. If I'm not there to poke fun at during regular work hours, they need something to do when they aren't in the shop or on the sales floor. I'm just surprised one of them knows how to write."

"You're hard to talk to when you get snarky," Walker says. "You're not going downtown on Easter. I don't know what the hell that's about, but it can't be good."

"Maybe I should go," Riley presses Walker. "You can come, too. We can investigate. Hamal might have something exciting planned. And what the hell else am I doing, besides trying to have sex with the stripper?"

Walker paces the room and wears a line into the plush carpeting with his dress shoes. "You're responsible for your own life, brother. You choose shit goals if you want. But forget Easter. Now get dressed in something other than sweats. If you want to bag the dancer, you've got to look proper."

Riley stands and stretches. He puts a slight amount of weight on his left heel and he's surprised when it doesn't collapse into pulsations of agony.

"I'll get my sexy shirt out. The one with the embroidery on the back of a saber tooth tiger skull."

"I thought you wanted to get laid," Walker teases and walks over to where the cards lay on the table. He points down at them with a stiff finger. "I don't know who Hamal is or what he's playing at, but you need to be careful with these assholes. First it's letters and then he'll be skinning your cat."

"I don't have a cat," Riley smirks.

"Laugh it up," Walker says and picks up a coffee table book. It's a heavy tome of vibrant pictures of Pacific Ocean islands. He places it over the three cards, hiding them completely. "All the world is a joke, right, Rye?"

"I'll be damned if it isn't," says Riley.

34   PEACH

The older woman's voice comes across the line, raspy from all her smoking but nasal because of the way she holds her nose aloft and pinched while addressing Peach. Although this time the woman in her early sixties sounds even more plugged up than usual.

"Another bout of bronchitis, Patti?" Peach asks the woman on the other end of the phone. It's her own way of playing at concern for the woman. There is no sickness in her other than her smoker's lungs and blackened heart. Peach wanders around her bedroom looking for a wayward earring. It's a black freshwater pearl and she's determined to find it and wear it out tonight.

Her phone beeps once and she tells the woman to hold on. She pulls the phone away and can see Linx is calling; the picture on the screen is a close up of his delicate face with patchy, black hair at his jawline. She'd taken the picture to prove to him he couldn't pull off a beard. Peach presses *decline* and goes back to her conversation.

"Sorry," she says and begins to explain but the woman cuts her off.

"More important than me? I don't want to be a bother to you, Peach."

"No, it was just Linx. I wasn't going to answer it. So, are you sick?"

The woman with the harsh voice coughs once and Peach knows it's more a forced display to curry sympathy than anything else. "I just don't know if Boise's warm enough for me yet."

"Then maybe you should stay in Orlando another month," Peach suggests. She looks under a magazine on her nightstand and digs around in a wooden box on her dresser carved with the image of two doves with their beaks holding on to one olive branch. No luck.

"You don't want me to come home?"

"I didn't say that, Patti. I think you should stay somewhere warm if you're ill."

The woman in Florida coughs again and then pauses. Peach is used to her lengthy silences. Peach believes Patti must think they lend a kind of gravitas or severity to a conversation. Peach finds the habit controlling, annoying and it tries her patience for Patti's antics.

"Or," she mutters, "come back to Boise. But I've got to go now. I'm going out in a few minutes."

"Do you have a date with a boy?"

"Not with a boy," Peach says and instantly regrets her word choice. "I mean, I'm just taking myself out tonight."

Peach flips over a bracelet sitting by the wooden box and the missing earring is no longer hidden underneath. She moves the phone to her other ear and pierces the sterling silver into the cavity in her earlobe.

"Just don't dress like a whore," Patti snips. "You dress like a whore and you're asking for trouble from men. And then it's no one's fault but yours."

And it's this nugget of wisdom which finally taxes Peach's patience. She lets Patti say demeaning things to her, make demands on her time and manipulate her with passive aggressive grandstanding. And while she won't tell the sixty-three year old woman off, Peach knows if she really does want to change her identity and control her life, she'll have to make some changes with Patti.

"I need to go. Let me know what you decide to do with your flight back to town. Bye, Patti."

The older woman harrumphs loudly on the other end of the phone. "What was that?"

"Bye, mother," Peach says and waits for the woman to say farewell. But Patti hangs up on her without a word.

She puts the phone on her dresser and walks to her closet. She's wearing a bright red set of matching underwear made out of delicate lace. Moving the tops and dresses around in her closet, she spies the dark green duffel in the back of the closet. Finally she decides on a button-down top in red gingham and a pencil skirt that sits high on her waist and emphasizes her curves. She pulls on the shirt and buttons it all the way to her collarbone. Then she unbuttons it to the place where her bra peeks over the checked fabric, her cleavage pointing to the bloodstone pendant around her neck. Every time she dresses, she's becoming more comfortable with showing skin.

The black pearl she shoved through her ear causes her flesh to pulse on her earlobe. She knows the flesh reddens there and an itch flares.

"Irritations," she says while pulling out the earring and making for her bathroom and some antibiotic ointment. "The black pearls of my life."

35 RILEY

He holds up the two dollar bill. He gets them special, just for his trips to Blaze Lounge. Riley thinks they're a classier way of tipping a stripper. Nell's gyrations are worth more than a dollar to him. A crisp two dollar is only right. And not just one. He has three in his hand and he's belly up to the stage on his crutches, waving the odd bills at the redhead.

She ignores him completely and moves to another area of the platform.

Walker slaps Riley on the back. "Well, if she won't take your money she's not likely to take your dick."

Riley jams the bills into his pocket, forgoing his wallet. He'll try again when he can get another drink in him. He might just scale the stage and force the money in the spandex boy shorts with red, sparkly trim.

"I'm not drunk enough," Riley says and scans the room for a table. His foot hurts despite his new habit of combining his OxyContin and whiskey. He needs to take a seat for a bit and use his head more than his finances to get Nell's attention.

At the bar sits Sev, a cheap Bic ballpoint pen hanging from his mouth and a row of napkins in front of his pint of porter. Riley decides he needs more alcohol and a visit with the overprotective boyfriend whom he plans on cuckolding.

Walker looks over at the bar as well. Riley watches his friend's eyes. Walker seems to sense his intentions and acts to defuse a potential brawl. "No way you're going up there. Find us a place to sit."

As he moves away, Riley wishes Walker didn't know him so well. He feels like he can't surprise anyone anymore. That he's too staid and predictable. He looks around the room again. Blaze Lounge is packed. A group of men play darts in a far corner and every table is occupied with at least one man leering at the girls on stage or receiving his own dance up close and personal.

Then he sees her. There's a woman in the back of the room. She's alone, her body squared to the stage. The colored lights aren't angled to hit that portion of the bar so she's nothing more than a shadow to Riley. But there are two empty seats at her table. And if he can't get lucky with Nell, he might score with the only female patron of the strip club.

He moves slowly to the table, tucking his crutches in tight as he shimmies around chairs and laughing, drunken pairs and trios of men. He decides the kind of woman who comes to Blaze Lounge is likely the kind who would give him a blowjob in the bathroom or at least show him her tits. And they would be without pasties. Riley begins to like his odds.

The woman stares straight ahead, oblivious to Riley standing to her side. She has long, blondish hair and a short torso. Her eyes are light, her lips thin. She's a little underweight, the bones of her face sharp and pronounced. Riley takes notice of her unbuttoned top and smiles.

"These seats available?" he asks, donning his most cherubic

grin.

She jumps in her seat, clears the vinyl cushion padding by a few inches. The woman's face is a mask of surprise, her eyes open so wide that her irises are islands in a sea of white. He can see her swallow.

"Oh shit," she exclaims before regaining her composure. The girl looks to the empty chairs at the table. She doesn't say anything for a moment and Riley assumes she's trying to think of a reason he can't sit down.

"It's just that my foot is hurt and I could really use a seat. I promise I won't bother you. I'm just here for the show."

He doesn't wait for an answer and uses his crutches held together to help lower his body to the chair nearest the woman. She turns her crossed legs away from him, points them right to the hallway leading to the bathrooms, and shifts her body so less of her form is in the sliver of light cutting across the cocktail table.

Walker is chatting up one of the barmaids, his elbow propped on the bar. Riley watches him puff out his chest and laugh at everything the woman says. He doesn't have drinks in front of him yet. Sev isn't at the bar anymore. His trail of napkins sits alone on the dark walnut bar top.

"Is he bothering you?" A deep voice comes from behind Riley and he turns his body to see Sev looming over the woman. He's wearing a striped t-shirt and the alternating lines of color make his chest seem even more massive.

"It's okay," the lady says and smiles at Sev, doing her best not to acknowledge Riley. "He just needs a place to sit and rest."

"All right, enchantress." He moves back to the bar and passes Riley, knocking his shoulder with his hip and looking down on him.

"Behave," he commands.

Riley shows his teeth and flips the man off once his back is turned. He eyes up the woman but she keeps her head turned away from him.

"He's right about you being an enchantress."

The woman rubs at her temples with her thumbs. "I don't think so. He's a snake, that one."

Riley tries out the name Sev the Snake in his head a few times and decides he likes it.

"I like you," Riley mumbles to the woman. Whiskey always puts him in a place between affection and lust. He's nearly a fifth in. If he can't lock it down with Nell tonight, this woman might be a fair substitute. The shape of her breasts under her top reminds him of two pomelos heavy with juice. Suddenly, his tongue craves the taste of citrus.

The woman says nothing in response. But her lips betray her, turning up at the corners.

36 PEACH

She wasn't expecting company at her table. And when she saw him approach she hoped he was moving toward the men's bathroom down the hallway behind her table. So when he spoke to her and asked to have a seat, she was mentally unprepared for the meeting. He smells rank to her, of some sort of pungent booze tainting each breath he expels. Yet there is an appeal to his bold character and his no-shits-given attitude to just hunker down in her space. She'd like those personality traits herself. In fact, they are some of the qualities she aims to cultivate during her personal renaissance.

There were many names she could use for the man with the crutches sitting next to her at the table. As she keeps her gaze on Nell dancing on the stage, she can see out of the corner of her eye as much as he tries to sneak glances at her cleavage, his real focus is on Nell as well. The stripper does a gliding leap onto the pole and spins down it like a winged seed off a maple tree.

There is only one name for the man at her table right now.

Competitor.

"I really do like you," he repeats and Peach sighs, picks up the glass of ice water in front of her. There's another drink, a Long Island Iced Tea on the table in a tall, clear tumbler. She ordered it so she could tip the waitress. The ice in it has long since melted, the alcohol never touching her lips.

Then the other man comes to the table. He doesn't have drinks in hand but his shirt is bright, even in the dim of the club, and he carries himself like his balls are made of gold and justifiably weighty. He tips his chin at Peach and speaks to the cripple.

"Who's your friend?"

"I don't know," the seated, drunk man says and sticks out a hand to Peach. "I'm Riley."

She returns his grasp briefly, extending her hand across her body but moving nothing else. "Nice to meet you."

Riley makes a face at his friend and the man in the vivid pinkish red shirt chuckles. Peach takes a passing glance at his face and notes how orange he looks from his fake tan. He sits at the other empty chair and proceeds to chat with his friend, shouting loudly across the table, leaning his body in front of Peach's view.

"Rye, you're not in there tonight. Let's move on. Plus the boyfriend's here. Means you've got less than a zero chance."

The man with the bum foot licks his lips and nods his head toward Peach. She can feel his attention on her though she doesn't look directly at him.

"I'm getting a tattoo," he exclaims to her and his friend.

"No way," the man to her left says. "Since when?"

Riley moves his hair from his eyes and reaches over to the abandoned Long Island. He takes a swig and watches Peach for a reaction. She keeps a stony countenance.

"I've got an appointment. I scheduled it. For tonight."

"Rye, you're wasted and making shit up."

He drinks more of the Long Island and touches Peach on the shoulder. She feels like she's just touched an electrified piece of metal. The energy discharges into her body. A zippy shock zings through her, to her heart and then out her feet.

"Want to come with? To see me get a tattoo?"

He pulls back his hand and when he does, she shakes out her arm. It tingles but she stops herself from standing up and running. Her breath is shallow. Her heartbeat quickens. She wants nothing more than to flee.

"No, sorry," she eventually speaks. "Can't stand the sight of blood."

"A girlie girl," the friend says, never introducing himself to Peach. She can venture a guess at his name but the less she engages the better.

"Nah, I get it," Riley quips. "You're here for the dancers." Then he yells across the table to his friend. "I've got to stop hitting on dykes."

Peach openly laughs at this. If only he knew how outlandish it was for him to try and pick her up. He is clueless. She imagines him in the childhood parable about the little Dutch boy with his finger in the dyke, trying to hold back the power contained there. There is no way for him to succeed. His digit will snap under all that water's energy.

The boys eventually gather up the gumption to stand, to escape the table and her cool attitude. They say nothing to Peach as they leave and she's happy for it. On their way out the club, the man named Riley tries to give Nell money one last time. This time she doesn't ignore him. Instead, she snatches the money from his fist and tosses it back out onto the tables ringed with clusters of lustful men. Peach watches Riley as this happens. She can see, from where she hides in the back of the lounge, how his body leans toward the stripper, his eyes narrow and he puts his hands to his sides, palms open.

Peach knows the man wants Nell more than ever now.

Competitor. They leave the bar and a minute later, Peach stands and makes her way past the stage. She doesn't hold out any cash for the stripper, but Nell whistles as Peach moves toward the entrance and Peach gives her a smile, wiggles her fingers at her.

Now Peach knows there will be no competition. Her cheeks give response, blushing deeply as she moves past the bouncer at the door. She hopes to find the two men in the parking lot as she exits the padded door. That boldness she so covets is blooming within and she wants them to see her strut out of the club, her eyes sparkling and her shoulders square. Those men might be enthralled to the passions contained by the walls of Blaze Lounge but Peach is not. She looks for them, sees them whooping like chimpanzees proud of their tool-making abilities as they slouch into a petite sports car. No matter if they cannot see her. She can see herself and knows what she must look like. Like the running, neon fire capping the building, like the glitter in Nell's tiny shorts, like the poems flowing out Sev.

37   RILEY

Riley and Walker are greeted by darkness. It's nearly nine
at night and the sign on the tattoo shop is no longer up-lit by
white light. A man in baggy black jeans and a polo shirt buttoned
up to his neck waits in the open doorway. He puffs a stream of
white smoke into the air, ditches his joint and waves the men
inside.

"You're Riley?" the tattooist asks, points at Walker.

"The other guy," Walker says. He helps Riley out of the car
without his crutches because Riley is insistent on leaving them
behind. Riley leans some of his weight on the shoulder of his
friend though Walker has a few inches on him in height. He
thinks they must look like they're about to perform some sort of
slapstick comedy one-off for the man in front of them. The
tattooist digs a toothpick out of his pants pocket and picks at his
teeth. When he moves, Riley can smell the marijuana on the
man's clothes.

"Nah, I don't ink anyone drunk."

"I have an appointment," Riley objects. "And you're high. But I still want you to give me a tattoo. You're the best I've seen. And I've had a lot of time to do research on the internet."

The man chews on the sliver of wood and steps aside to let the men in. "It's only a maintenance smoke. See, I'm what people might call addicted. Now why you want me giving you a permanent knowing all that?"

Riley enters first with tender steps on his left heel, followed by Walker, his arms outstretched, moving behind Riley like he's seeing the first uneasy steps of a toddler. The tattooist stays in the doorway, his back to a street light across the parking lot. His torso and head glow with a fuzzy white aura.

"I'm an addict, too," Riley says and steadies himself at the front counter. An antiquated cash register is on the corner of a glass case containing metal barbs and rings of varying shapes and colors, ready to be plunged into holes in the head or the genitals.

"No doubt," the tattooist says and shuts the door. "I could smell you before I could see you. I'm guessing you're a whiskey drinker."

"But I'm not an alcoholic. That's not my addiction."

Riley takes his wallet out and checks his money fold. "You accept credit?"

"It's pussy, ain't it?" the man hazards a guess at Riley's addiction. Walker coughs and Riley leaves his wallet on the glass countertop.

"Do I need to sign papers or something?" He glances around the counter. His foot feels fabulous, but his head pounds, the shop dipping and heaving like the prow of a ship.

The tattooist walks behind the counter and produces a clipboard with a few papers on it. He clicks on a pen he pulls from the metal claw at the top of the particleboard.

"Just sign. Won't do you no good to read it as liquored up as you are."

Riley's signature is a messy scrawl of a capital R followed by three loops. He signs all the papers and tosses the clipboard down on the counter. It knocks over a small display of rolling papers and lighters with casings covered in little green men and psychedelic whirls.

"Get him to my chair," the man points to Walker and then motions to a spot a few feet away from the front counter. It's an old barber's chair; the arms are covered in foam and blue vinyl and there's a silver footrest at the bottom of the seat worn smooth in places from the thousands of soles rubbed there over decades of use.

"I'm Roman," the tattooist says. Riley gets into the chair without Walker's help and watches the man snap on a pair of surgical gloves, just like the ER doctor pulled on when examining his crushed toes. "And I'll be your tattooist this evening."

Riley closes his eyes and imagines the man for a moment as a Roman soldier, a plume of red running down his metal helmet and a short sword with a pommel capped in an iron sphere at his waist. Has the soldier been ordered to kill or does he fight for his own reasons, perhaps at the behest of his own god? Like Mars or Zeus or another violence-loving taskmaster?

Roman stands with his hands in the air, like he's about to walk into a delivery room and escort a baby into the world. He sucks at his tongue until Riley opens back up his eyes. "What and where?"

Lifting his pelvis, Riley pulls out a piece of paper from his pocket and hands it to Roman. The tattooist takes in the image and when Walker tries to peek at it over the man's shoulder, Riley shouts at him to wait and see the final product. Walker plays nice and walks away, scrolls through old text messages on his phone.

"This it? You don't need an artist for this. Someone else would have charged you less. Just like this? No color?"

Roman hands the paper back to Riley and snaps on a pair of black nitrile gloves. He fills an ink cup from a larger squeeze bottle of black, viscous liquid and retrieves needles from a small cabinet near the chair. He peels the wrapping off the slivers of metal and lays out his tools on a wheeled tray with a paper liner.

The sweet coat of whiskey in Riley's throat makes him feel secure and contented. He used to hate the idea of tattoos but now he feels like he needs this particular image on his body. It's part of his quest to reclaim his manhood. It'll be something to show Nell. He supposes she's the type of girl who likes body ink.

"No color. Well, not yet. And I want it on my foot."

Roman looks down at the foot rest and takes in Riley's bandaged left foot.

"I'm not inking over scabs, man. It better be your right foot."

Riley brings his leg up and perches his heel on the edge of the blue vinyl seat. He finds the edge of the gauze bandaging and begins to unroll it from his ankle. Normally he would keep it in a tight bundle as he unwinds, but the alcohol causes him to be sloppy and unsteady. When he gets to the last of the cotton swaddling his toes, he lets the bandaging fall to the floor.

The end of his foot is trimmed with a set of black knots that look like ties made out of dark fishing line. The meat of his foot is still dark purple. Where the top of his foot begins to curve up to his ankle, Riley points and nods. There is little flesh there; nerves, tendon and bone will absorb the pain delivered via tattoo gun.

"Right there will be good," and then he hiccoughs five times before holding his breath and willing his diaphragm to relax.

Roman picks up his tattooing needle and attaches it to the ink base. He flicks a switch and the contraption buzzes to life. He pulls a squat, wheeled stool toward him and takes a seat. "This'll hurt like fuck, man."

Riley comes back with a reasonable retort. "Just lost five toes. Think I can handle it."

The first prick reminds Riley of stepping on pine needles when he was young, running around the family's favorite campsite near Redfish Lake. The after-burn of the sap and pollen zooming through the bloodstream caused massive itching and swelling. He doesn't watch Roman at his work but sits back flush in the chair and thinks of summers on the unspoiled lake near the Sawtooth Mountains.

A moment later, the needle clicks off and Roman swears, pulls a wad of tissue out of a box of Kleenex perched on the tray of supplies and dabs at the foot.

"This is why I don't tattoo drunks. Your blood's too thin, man. I can't see what I'm doing in this mess. You'll have to reschedule."

Riley looks down and can see the barest line of black running down the slope of his foot, hidden by a steady flow from the opened pores.

"It's not like I'll bleed out," Riley pleads. Walker pulls his attention away from his phone and comes over to look.

"I'm just punching through the epidermis, but all this blood ain't good. You shouldn't be bleeding like this with me shooting ink into you. A little blood is okay. A lot is a problem. Blood and ink don't mix." Roman sets his needle down on the tray and pushes his wheeled stool away from Riley.

Riley knows arguing won't get him what he wants. Then, the flavor of a beef hotdog, held over a campfire, spitted on a branch of peeled willow flares across his tongue and he's back to his memories of summer.

"Okay," he mumbles, "I'll come back. I want this design, came up with it myself. I'll come back for you, Roman centurion. "

"What the hell you call me?"

"Don't be offended. It's a good thing," he tells the man

before reaching out and patting him on his forearm. "For the empire! For Rome!"

38   PEACH

The little Miata wasn't hard to follow in the light traffic of a Boise evening. The men drove slowly, hip hop blasting from their open windows. The crippled one hung his good foot out the window, shaking it to the beat of the bass drum.

Peach kept her distance when they pulled into a little strip mall on the bench of land overlooking downtown, full of residences, ethnic markets and dive bars. It was the shelf of land where her home sat, too. She drove into the same narrow parking lot, but shut off her engine a few doors down from their destination.

A man was waiting for them at the tattoo parlor. Peach had to squint to see the name of the shop. The sign wasn't illuminated and it took a moment for her eyes to adjust so she could pick out the letters and form them into words with meaning. *Crucible Tattoo.*

She smiled right then. She still smiles as she sits in her small Honda Civic. She doesn't know what she's waiting for.

Going into the shop is out of the question and she wonders if she should go back and watch Nell do another dance. She considers the men might go back to the strip club after the tattooing and this both exhilarates and frustrates her.

Her purse, a small white and gray square, vibrates on the passenger side seat. She pulls out her phone. It's Linx again. But this time she doesn't hit the decline button. She lets it vibrate on silent until her voicemail clicks on. Then she digs around in the bag and pulls out a Mars bar, unwraps it and takes two large bites, savoring the chocolate on her teeth.

Rolling down her window, she watches the front of the tattoo parlor and wonders what the man named Riley is having done to his skin. What could be so tantalizing in form he felt it needed to be drawn on his flesh for the rest of his life? It must be something special or important to make such a late appointment. She understands how when you want something done to your body, you do it, no matter the cost. It's as if art possesses humans, entire societies, once a symbol or sign is considered beloved.

Perhaps, she considers, he's commemorating something. A victory? A new path in life? He didn't look the type to get a tattoo. He was clean shaven, hair long enough to slick back but not quite long enough to put in a ponytail yet. He wore dress pants and a nice, black patent on his right foot.

Peach doesn't know what he's getting done or why, but she's proud of herself for following him to the tattoo shop. When she set out after them, her heart beat wildly, her eyes darting around at every intersection and stop sign. Now she feels in charge. Her body is relaxed, the chill air seeping into her car doing little to chill the warm blood running through her.

The man she saw greet the boys outside the shop was striking enough. Peach can sense the distant suns overhead through the metal roof of her Honda. They make a suggestion. So she closes her eyes for a moment and commits the man's face to memory. She thinks of what she might want if she can't have Nell. Perhaps a tattoo. Or even the tattooist. It all depends. She will look into this place, find the man's information and portfolio online. It will be part of her personal education. It may create options.

She undoes her seatbelt and cranes her head outside the window. The stars are mere suggestions of light against the heavily lit parking lot. She wishes her short term paramour, the star she wishes to speak to now, was overhead.

"It's called Crucible Tattoo," she whispers to the universe. "It couldn't be more perfect."

SATURDAY, THE 4TH OF APRIL, 2015

39   RILEY

"So he has me down for an appointment then? He's the only one that can do it, okay?" Riley asks into the phone. His head is pinched, right at the center of his temples and the morning coffee and slabs of bacon have done little to ease his hangover. Worse yet, his left foot is flush with pain in another place now, thanks to the addition of a line of ink down the front of his ankle.

"You scheduled last night. Nothing has changed in the last twelve hours." The woman on the other end has a clipped edge to her voice. "Anything else?"

"No," Riley says. "Thank you."

He hangs up and puts down his coffee. It's lukewarm and needs a nuke in the microwave. But he suddenly doesn't have the stomach for more food or drink and he decides to go outside instead.

This time he doesn't force his foot into a snow boot and use his old footbag as ballast. It does feel markedly different; his missing toes make his left foot lighter and his center of gravity while walking is affected. He's still dependent on stable things like tree trunks and door frames or his arms held out to his sides as if he looks ready for a game of airplane. Instead of trying to compensate for his missing appendages, he pulls a roll of saran wrap from a kitchen drawer and spins the clear plastic around his bandaged foot.

He has very vague memories of last night. He remembers the blood when he looked down to see how the tattoo was coming and then the ride home, Walker helping him inside and re-bandaging his foot. But before that, the time at Blaze Lounge, is a fuzzy blur. He thinks he may have hit on a woman other than Nell but he can't be sure. He cannot recall the woman's hair or figure to mind. She is nothing more than a sense of the feminine without any definition.

When his foot is bound in plastic wrap, he slips a runner on his good foot and takes his time walking down the driveway. He passes the place he fell when he tried to run. He thinks if he concentrates on using just the heel of his left foot, he'll be done with the crutches in no time. But today, he'll take them along. The morning sun hasn't warmed the day yet and clouds moving in from the west allude to a light rain. In the yard across his street, purple tulips flank spots of bright yellow daffodils.

He shuffles along on his crutches, challenging himself to put more weight on his left foot every ten steps. When he gets a few houses down the street, his weight is almost divided fifty-fifty on his feet. A shock of color catches his eye at the curb by a single-story house. There, in a clump of ratty yellow and green grass is a plastic Easter egg of brilliant orange.

A man calls at Riley from across the lawn. He has a pale pink Easter basket in the crook of his arm. It's full of other brightly colored eggs. He pokes his hands in bushes and trees, leaving spots of color as he moves.

"I know you want the malt balls in that egg but leave it there," the man jokes and keeps on with his job of hiding eggs.

Riley stops and watches the man plant a blue oval in a mess of deep purple grape hyacinths, their tiny flowers creeping up stalks, clustered together like a pyramidal cap.

"Easter is on Sunday," Riley suggests. "Think you're a day early. Not sure about the dollar short part, though."

His neighbor stops and puts the basket down on the grass. He's wearing open-toed sandals and a sun visor. "I know, but I only get the kids today. Their mom's taking them to brunch tomorrow and church. Hell of the thing is one of my kids is fifteen. And he still wants to search for plastic eggs full of candy on the front lawn." The father shakes his head. "He never gets tired of it. Wants it every year."

Riley can imagine a teenager, tall and gangly, pushing a young sibling out of the way to snatch up all the candy for himself. He wishes he could have had Easter egg hunts when he was a teenager. But after he got out of grade school, he was limited to dying white eggs with his mother, dipping them in cups of vivid pigments, hot water and white vinegar. He can remember the smell of acid, the crackle as the shells were lowered into the coffee mugs.

"Easter egg hunting sounds fun," he says, but sees the man isn't listening as much as he is venting.

"I told their mother I wanted them this year for Easter. But she just had to schedule away their Sunday. But I suppose we don't get to choose when the hunt is on, eh? I guess the hunt just starts when the fox breaks out of a bush and begins to run. So a Saturday Easter Egg Hunt. I guess it is what it is."

The man picks back up his basket and resumes his tucking of plastic eggs into hidey-holes and mounds of vegetation. Riley turns around and heads back home when a steady patter of rain drops from the firmament above him, turning his blond hair brown from wetness. This time, with every ten steps, he puts less weight on his left foot, careful to not let the rubber nubs on the ends of his crutches slip on wet leaves or get stuck in softened mud. It's like the rainwater makes him feel less capable and sure of his foot so he doesn't expect anything of it anymore. He retracts his dependence on it until he reaches his front door and it swings freely from his ankle, doing nothing at all.

40   PEACH

She spent the afternoon chatting with Linx over the phone, setting up plans for Easter morning, and when she finally ends the conversation, the sun is waning in power and dipping low. She has significant, potent work to do. If she leaves her apartment now, she might even catch sight of her star in the sky if she is truly lucky, truly blessed. Peach figures the trip will take her a few hours including driving, waiting, acting. She wants to leave soon, get a little sleep in the car before carrying out her task, observe the environs long enough to make sure everything is as it should be. The return home isn't of much concern to her currently. She hopes the process will be invigorating, completed with aplomb, and then she will take her time getting home, simmering in the spectacular events of the evening.

"Another bold step. Another bit of ritual," she says to her empty apartment. Peach thinks it a good sign if she is sure of the success of her outing before it has even begun.

She goes to her bedroom and opens her closet. There lies

152

the dark green duffel bag. It's the same bag she took out the night she forced Linx out of her apartment and took to the streets with the joke stuck in her mind of going out for a run. She pulls it out and unzips it, checks its contents. A few things are needed and she makes a mental list of what she must dig out from other parts of her apartment and add to the bag.

Her dark wool hoodie slips off a hanger easily and she swings it on. She's cleaned it the best she could of her vomit and the red specks of color. Then she tugs on the end of her wig and it comes off, the synthetic netting scraping her scalp. The itching has been intense for the past few days and she's glad to be free of it. She lays the blonde wig on her pillow, spreads out the hair and looks at the way it flows over her pillowcase. Lying against the white sheets on her bed, it's beautiful. She realizes she must be beautiful when she's wearing it. She leaves it there, as if she cares to collect the scalp of her former self. Because the wig is representative of just that: her former self. Old Peach. And she's taken it off for tonight and someday, for good.

She checks to see if her bloodstone pendant is still around her neck. Of course it's there; she never takes it off. She tells herself she would feel its weight leave her collarbone if the chain were to break and the stone were to fall.

"You are like the engine outside my body, friend," she speaks down to the rock. "You and the others present at this time." She looks around her bedroom again before snatching up her work bag, rolling back her shoulders, and saying goodbye to a room empty of another living soul.

SUNDAY, THE 5TH OF APRIL, 2015

SUNDAY, THE 5TH OF APRIL, 2015

41　　　　　　　　　　RILEY

No matter how he argues the merit of his intended action, Walker won't go downtown with Riley, at the behest of a card, on Easter morning. He badgered him yesterday after his hangover had subsided and left Walker a voicemail at six this morning. But he'd heard nothing from his friend. So Riley knew if he wanted to get downtown to see whatever it was this Hamal wanted him to see, he would have to do it alone.

He curses himself for owning an SUV. The vehicle is high, not as tall as Double Al's Dodge Ram, but the Nissan requires him to step up and in and he's happy at least he can put his right foot in first and pull up his body with the handlebar over the door.

He makes a game of counting the number of churches he passes between his home and the Basque Block downtown. He notes seven, all of them with front entrances flung open and people flowing inside. One is bedecked in a garland of fake, white lilies. At a stop sign, sweat beading at his temples, he hears the distinctive bellow of an organ coming from another church. The singing voices of parishioners compete against the sonorous pipes.

During his journey downtown, he panics at every stop light. He's lucky his vehicle isn't a manual transmission. But this does little to calm his anxiousness when he needs to push on the brake or the gas. All these presses are done with the right foot, but Riley works himself into a mild sweat, wondering if he'll get a rare charley horse in his right foot and be forced to maneuver the pedals with his wounded left foot. He'd surely crash into a median or rear-end a worshipper on his way to pray. So he takes the drive slowly, decreasing speed before each green light, getting honked at by two cars at one intersection.

It takes him fifteen minutes to get downtown from his home in the residential area of southeast Boise. He hooks a right on Capitol Boulevard, a wide one-way expanse that leads straight to the steps of the white marble of Idaho's capitol building. He hits a major cross street at Capitol and Myrtle and spots orange barriers a half block in front of his vehicle. Behind the barricades are stretches of roads without cars. Police cars, new Dodge Chargers, are spread out downtown, their red and blue lights whirling in the early morning sun, sirens turned off.

Riley keeps going forward, through the intersection and as close as he can drive up to one of the heavy plastic barricades before he can hang a left or right and try and work his way around the blocked off area. He frowns and flips down his visor. The Basque Block, an area of cultural and ethnic pride for Boise's Basques, is only a few blocks away. He wanted to park as close as possible, maybe even leave his crutches in his car.

A police officer in a bright yellow vest lined with metallic deflectors steps from the sidewalk near one of the barricades and waves at Riley to stop his vehicle. The cop rubs his gloved hands together and Riley puts his car in park and rolls down his window. There aren't any cars behind him, the morning still young; those who are awake are either in church, hunting Easter Eggs or tucking into breakfast somewhere warm.

"Can I ask what's going on?" Riley smiles at the cop.

The man is young, likely fresh to his calling as a cop, and has a ratty moustache covering his upper lip.

"You're going to have to turn around. If you're trying to get north of here, you'll have to go down to 1st or up to 11th to get past the perimeter."

Riley clicks on the heat in his vehicle and rubs his finger over the bumps on his steering wheel.

"Right," he says, "but what's happening?"

And the officer doesn't need to open his mouth, because Riley gets to experience the answer to his question directly. A sheep, its white wool dirty and twisted, pushes through a gap between two of the orange barricades.

The officer swears and moves toward the animal, his arms outstretched. He hums loudly as he walks toward the sheep, doing his best to shoo it back through the gap and toward the city center.

Riley can see a hint of color on the sheep and when it turns sharply to avoid the movements of the cop, he sees it's been painted on one of its flanks. The number 73 seems to hover over the wool in deep red relief.

And there's something else. Riley pokes his head out of his SUV to get a better look at the sheep's head and neck before the cop is victorious and ushers the beast back into its corral. It looks as if a picture, maybe cut out of a magazine, hangs from the sheep's neck by a length of string.

Riley's gaze confirms it's a photograph. The image is of Heidi Klum, dazzling in a floor-length gown made in alternating layers of green and blue fabric.

The sheep is pushed back and the cop does his best to nudge the barriers closer together. They're heavy with bases full of water but he manages by throwing his thighs against the plastic.

Riley watches the entire thing, mouth slightly agape, until the cop comes back to the window of his Nissan.

The cop breathes heavily. "You should have seen number 49 with an old picture of Cheryl Tiegs around his neck," he says to Riley, then pauses to let out a string of tight sneezes. "He jumped five barricades before we could run him down. Can you believe that?"

42   PEACH

With hot lattes in hand and a bag of crusty almond
croissants ready to be eaten on a bench further downtown, Peach
and Linx stroll next to one another in the cool of the Easter
morning. Linx bumps into her as they walk and never
apologizes, even when the milky coffee in Peach's hand spills
over the lid and scalds her thumb.

"Knock it off," she pleads. "Can't we just walk in peace?"

She's cranky and tired. The work she did last night did not
afford her the luxury of napping in her car. Things had gone
smoothly enough, but she'd been harried by time and physical
limitations. Now she operates on the short high from her success
and the mild buzz one receives when they have been awake for
twenty-seven hours.

They pass a few office buildings, restaurants busying
themselves with prepping for the slam they'll get with the brunch
crowd. And then they hit barricades, circling the street in front of
them, enclosing the sidewalks and snaking across alleyways. For

as far as Peach can see running north and south, the heart of downtown Boise is under containment.

"What's this?" Linx asks. "And where are we going anyway?"

"I just wanted to walk. We don't always need a destination, do we?" She takes in the barriers for a moment longer and then pushes her coffee into Linx's hands and swings her legs over one of the rectangular plastic fences ballasted with liquid.

"Come on," she waves for him to deliver the food back into her hands and smiles. "Let's go see what's happening."

Linx hesitates and then shuffles his body on top of the barrier with the help of his hands and the hindrance of his short legs, and hops down to the other side. He gets a bit of dirt on his jeans and rubs at it until it comes away.

"You're the type to run from danger, not toward it," he says.

Peach hands him back his drink and the bag of pastries and proceeds forward, cautious of what she might find. Suddenly, it doesn't matter if her mind is running on pure adrenaline and minimal rest.

"Who knows if it's something dangerous, Linx? It could just be cordoned off for a parade later this morning, or a fun run. Maybe there's some fitness thing going on."

"On Easter morning?" he laughs, doubt obvious in his voice.

"Maybe everyone dons Easter Bunny costumes and hops a 5K?"

Linx pushes at her back in play as they walk forward and Peach does her best not to tense up. She can see him smiling and she doesn't want to disturb the moment of fun they're having together.

They walk on, east, passing other groups of early morning folks, many of them dressed in nice suits or skirts. Some of the people look distressed or confused and Peach stops herself from asking them what's so upsetting. She wants to discover it on her own, to take in whatever is happening to the people downtown with her own senses.

"Do you hear that?" she mumbles to Linx.

She turns and looks down Capitol Boulevard, toward the Basque Block where little restaurants serve paella and every few years Boise's sizable Basque population gathers to hoop dance during San Ignacio or Jaialdi.

She takes Linx's hand and he pulls back for a minute before letting her lead him down the sidewalk. She catches the sound of people, some shouting, others laughing. And under it all is the murmur of animal noise.

So when they turn the corner onto the cobblestone paving of the Basque Block, she's not surprised to hit more barricades with her thighs. And behind the barricades are dozens, if not hundreds of sheep milling about the block. Police officers do their best to keep them within the blockade, but sheep are jumping the orange fences and making their way down side streets.

In the concentrated chaos of the Basque Block, small groups of people hug their bodies to storefront windows and keep away from the sheep, their eyes glued to the strange display of animals in front of them. She wonders if they attempt to make sense of their lamb chops and wool sweaters taking over their urban streets.

Peach thinks of climbing the barriers here, too, but before she does, she hears the voice of a little girl, no more than seven or eight years old, a few feet away. She wears a lavender dress with a lace petticoat and a white bonnet on her head. The hat is made of straw; a ring of pink, blue and purple rosettes festoon the material. Pastel satin is tied in a droopy bow around her waist. The girl's face is glowing, her cheeks ruddy. And she points to one of the sheep, the beast vulnerable on the ground.

The sheep, a ewe, has her forelegs down flat on the pavers. She's louder than the rest of the sheep moving around, anxious for a place to hide or a means of escape. She has her docked, fuzzy tail in the air and from what Peach can see, the brown crescent tip of a hoof protrudes from her uterine opening.

The child giggles and tugs at her mother's hand. She does a little pirouette and exclaims so loudly some of the sheep surrounding her bolt to the other side of the street.

"It's the Lamb of God! Everyone, look at the Lamb of God!"

43   RILEY

The strangest thing about the scene he sees as he walks
toward the Basque Block, slowly making his way on his
crutches, the foamy cushions under his armpits wet with sweat,
is the way that people act. He watches as a woman in a white
dress and a green shawl walks cautiously up to individual sheep
and tries to pet their sides. Another man he passes on his way to
the epicenter of the chaos has two sheep backed into a corner
between a dumpster and an opened door. He's talking to them
like they're toddlers, trying to rationalize a course of events. He
tells them not to panic, that they'll be eating grass soon and then
he picks up his phone and calls someone for help.

When he gimps past a sheep with a number 92 painted on
its side—a tight shot of a woman with a blonde bob and wide,
red lips around its neck—he wonders how many sheep there
must be, confused and scared amongst the brick and metal of a
metropolitan setting.

He reaches the Basque Block and stands next to another

officer in the same bright yellow get-up with the reflective stripes the first cop he spoke with wore. He can see the cops are doing their best to keep the flock of sheep in one area. A large trailer is backing up down a side street close to the block and a few men in Carhartts and worn work shirts wave it toward the mass of animals. Two reporters are on the scene, large microphones clutched in their hands, video cameras pointed at them as they comment about the sheep and chat with onlookers tickled to be on camera.

Riley doesn't understand the numbers crudely painted on the sides of the sheep, or the pictures of women gracing their necks. But he considers that this is what Hamal wanted him to see. It's too coincidental to be otherwise. He doesn't understand the why of it though. Why release a bunch of frightened animals in downtown Boise just for him to look at the ensuing mess? The idea isn't just odd, it's overly cryptic. Riley tussles with the idea he's so important to someone else they would go to so much work on his account, especially such peculiar work. He doesn't know what to believe. But if it's true, if the livestock are there for him, he's certain the letters are no simple prank played by his coworkers.

He looks at the officer next to him. He stares straight ahead, his eyes focused on a group of sheep rubbing their heads against the bark of a small golden locust. If he told the man about the cards, about how someone wanted him downtown to see these sheep, that these animals might be here solely for him, the cop would laugh at him. At best he would tell him to shove off. At worse he'd give him a police escort to a hospital for a psych test.

So he says nothing. And as interesting as the scene is, Riley is hungry for a stack of pancakes covered in strawberries with a side of link sausages and a cup of coffee to go with his thoughts about this morning. He puts his weight back on his crutches, a parting serenade of *baas* in his ears as he hobbles toward an area of downtown free of domesticated animals.

44   PEACH

The lambing ewe is all the impetus Peach needs to clear the barricade in front of her. Linx calls after her but she ignores him. She's desperate to see the miracle unfold before her. She is sure it is a sign. New life for them all.

No one stands by the ewe kneeling on her front legs. Peach is the first to approach and as she does, she coos lightly to the ewe, doing her best not to upset the expectant mother. The ewe bleats and grinds her teeth. Her mouth hangs open, a thick grayish-pink tongue lolling out the side.

Peach moves around the back end of the animal and lifts the tail slightly to get a better look at what's happening. Now that she's close she can see the tip of a nose along with a second front hoof protruding from the vagina. She keeps herself from yelling out in surprise and joy and instead looks up to the piercing blue of the sky overhead and smiles.

The ewe drops to her hind legs without warning and Peach startles before regaining her focus. She sees Linx move up next to her, the coffees and pastries clutched to his chest. His face is white and stony.

"It's going to come out," Peach says and stands back. She looks around for something soft for the baby to rest upon and wishes she'd brought a heavier, down-filled coat. She decides she'll have to catch the lamb before it lands on the unyielding brick of the street.

With each contraction, the lamb emerges farther out of the ewe. The face of the lamb is calm, its eyes squeezed shut. Ten minutes later, Peach is easing its back legs free from the mother. The birth has been a success. A semicircle of onlookers have gathered to be witness to the process, keeping several feet back from the ewe. The girl in the lavender dress is among them. She grins widely at Peach and swings her skirt around her legs.

Peach runs her hands over the lamb, clearing some of the afterbirth from its wooly face. Its eyes open, striking in their blackness, and Peach gently carries the lamb, a female, to the side of the ewe and eases her under her body. The baby finds a teat and takes long draws of milk from her mother.

And then Peach notices the number painted on the side of the ewe. It's a fat number 8 in deep scarlet. She swallows hard.

She stands away then, waiting for the mother to regain her feet and let the lamb nurse more naturally. But the pained bleating continues, the ewe does not stand on her hooves, and Peach realizes she must be having twins.

Moving back around the sheep, she can see the tips of two hooves emerging, solid and sharp. But this time there is no length of nose accompanying them and when the ewe gives a strong push, Peach can see how the hooves tilt slightly upwards. The lamb is coming out backwards and face down.

"I've got to do something," she says to Linx.

"Let it be, Peach," he cautions, but she is already digging around in her purse. She pulls out a small bottle of hand sanitizer and unscrews the cap. She dumps the contents of clear, gelatinous alcohol over her hands and forearms, rubbing it into her skin. The smell makes her cringe, the fumes overwhelming her sinuses. She knows it's better than nothing.

She slips one hand into the ewe and Linx exclaims behind her.

"Oh God, you've gone insane."

She can feel the backside of the lamb but she can't get a good hold of the legs. So she pushes in her other arm and locates the pelvis with her hands. Not sure of what to do at this point, Peach kneels behind the sheep and glances at the lamb nursing strongly on the laboring ewe.

Perfect Peach can do this, she thinks. She knows that this is part of her flowering life. That she's meant to be here, now, helping this ewe give birth. This animal is her responsibility and she will see to this taxing labor.

The uterine walls contract, squeeze against Peach's hands and she can feel the baby shift slightly toward her. She waits and when she feels the contraction again, she pulls gently on the back legs of the lamb, careful not to tug so roughly that she'll dislocate a joint or two.

Sitting with crossed legs behind the sheep, Peach finally pulls the second lamb into the cool air of Easter morning and swabs off its face with her palms, sticky and wet with birthing fluid. The lamb doesn't suck in air at first. But after a moment, it pries open its small mouth and flares its nostrils.

Peach checks its sex and sees that it's male. She bursts into tears and her sobs become uncontrollable.

Instead of placing the ram down underneath the ewe, she stands with him still in her arms, his shaky legs dangling from her embrace. Now she understands why she did what she did last night, why she took what she took.

And then, without plan or thought, Peach runs to one of the barricades. She shuffles her body up and over, legs wide and splayed, and flees down the street, away from the other sheep.

The heartbeat of the animal held close to her core thumps in time with her own. She can hear Linx calling for her to come back. She can hear the little girl let out a scream followed by loud sobs of confusion and anger over the stolen Easter miracle.

45 RILEY

The carbs from the pancakes and the greasy meat have made him sleepy, but instead of heading for his bedroom and catching a late morning nap, Riley decides he better call one of the two people who need to hear about his accident. He presses his phone to his ear after dialing and takes a deep breath, keeps his eyes fixated on the drawing hanging on his refrigerator.

She picks up after one ring, her voice light at first and heavier upon hearing who's calling.

"He's playing with his Easter toys right now," Kristin says and then yells at someone in the background, saying something about rolls of paper towels.

"It's Easter, Kristin. I just want to talk to him for a second," Riley responds. He keeps his voice mellow and quiet. He doesn't want the exchange with his ex to be more wrathful than necessary.

"Right, one of the only days out of the year you *do* want to talk to your son."

Riley keeps himself from saying something snide about the boy's possible parentage. But even though he keeps silent, it does him no good. Kristin seems to know his thoughts, despite his lack of words.

"Go to hell, Riley. I'll get him on the line."

A high-pitched voice, small and distracted, comes on the line.

"Hi, Riley."

He can't believe the boy is five-years-old. Soon he'll be able to have longer conversations with him, talk about sports and girls. Then the kid will be shaving hair from his chin and driving a used car too fast down the highway.

"Hey, buddy. What toys are you playing with?"

"Mom got me a blue chicken for Easter. Did you see it?"

Riley is thrown by the question. Kristin and Tate don't live in Boise, but then he recalls how his mind worked when he was that young. The world was small and all the people you knew were in the same area. Distance meant nothing, nor did complicated relationships. Tate might even think Riley and his mother are actual friends.

"No, I didn't. You'll have to show it to me next time I see you."

"When is that gonna be?" the boy asks and his voice gets far away. Riley can tell he's pulled the phone away from his mouth.

"Soon, I'm sure." Riley tries to find it within him to say something about the accident. But he doesn't know how to tell a young child that he's missing all the toes on his left foot. No matter how often he rehearsed this call when he was drunk on Jameson or Maker's Mark these past afternoons, now, with Tate on the phone, he knows it's not the time.

He smiles into the phone and imagines the boy's light hair with the curls at his neck and his hazel eyes. He wonders if he's gotten any taller, wider, smarter since he'd seen him last.

"You have a good Easter, okay? I just wanted to call and

say hello. Eat a bunch of those sugary marshmallow chicks for me."

"Okay," Tate says absently, distracted by something. "Me and the man will have fun with the blue chicken. I promised him I'd share everything with him."

Riley's brow creases. "The man. Do you mean Brian, your stepdad?"

"No, I mean the man," Tate repeats and then sings a Sesame Street tune about being a good friend. "If you come visit me, you can be friends with the man, too."

Riley runs his eyes over the picture of the golden eagle Tate drew. Its flat, lifeless eyes stare back.

"Okay, little dude. We can all play with the blue chicken together the next time I see you. It's a deal."

"You want to talk to mom again?"

"No," Riley says, "I only called to talk to you. "

Later, after the talk with Tate, Riley considers calling the other person he'd avoided telling about his accident. But he decides against it. He figures she'll be eating Easter dinner with her family, shallow dishes of *camarones* and *langosta* arrayed on card tables, the house alive with the voices of fifty relatives and friends. Maybe the voice of a new boyfriend. And Riley knows, as bitter as it makes him to hear Kristin's voice, it would be nothing compared to hearing the deep timber of a stranger speak over the line connected to a number he used to adore calling.

"Mayra Vega Pena," he says her name and continues on with his mock conversation while opening his fridge and hunting for more food, though he isn't hungry. The drawing from Tate is no longer in his line of sight. He smells cabbage rotting in his produce bin. "I have something to tell you about my toes."

46 PEACH

The lamb is limp and weak by the time Peach gets him into her apartment. As she walks by her couch on her way to the kitchen, she snatches a quilt off the back cushions. It was something she picked up at a thrift store a few years back. Whenever she had friends over, which was very rare, they would ask if it had been made special for her by an aunt or grandmother. Peach would tell them it was from her mother, that Peach had even picked out the colors, the red and orange blocks stitched together. But it was all a lie. It meant nothing to her. It was a blanket.

She tosses it on the kitchen floor and gently lays down the newborn lamb. Linx bursts through the front door and slams it behind him.

"You've lost your balls," he yells at Peach, but she doesn't stop moving to argue with him. She considers him lucky to have caught up to her, getting in her little Honda before she drove off, screaming at her the entire drive back to her apartment. She would have left him downtown otherwise.

"The expression is 'lost your marbles.' It has nothing to do with balls. And please don't yell around the lamb," she says and opens the refrigerator. She rearranges some green olives, a jug of guava juice and produces a glass bottle of whitish-yellow liquid. She pours a bit into a smaller glass and heats it in the microwave for thirty seconds.

She snaps her fingers at Linx. "Get in the second drawer down by the oven and bring me that plastic funnel."

He does what she says, a look of confusion on his face. "Why the hell do you have yellow milk in your fridge?"

"It's colostrum," she says, the only explanation she'll offer up. "And the lamb needs it." She did not question the stars, especially her best, lovely star, when they murmured to her the dictate to get the nutrient-rich milk. She had obeyed, confused at the time, though their commandment now had meaning.

She snatches the funnel from his hands and pulls the milk from the microwave. She dribbles a bit on her wrist, the way she's seen mothers test the milk for their infants, and is satisfied it's not too hot for the lamb's mouth.

The animal is quiet, eyes rolling around, taking in the colors and shapes of the kitchen. Peach gently pushes the tip of the plastic funnel into the small ram's mouth and drips a bit of the warmed milk onto his tongue. His eyes snap forward, locking onto the funnel and he sucks down all the milk he's given.

"I'll have to get a livestock bottle later today at that farm store," Peach says.

"What the hell are you doing?"

Peach is in love with the way the lamb kneads at the tip of the funnel with his lips. He has heavily lashed eyes. He smells like warm cream though his wool is covered in putrid secretions.

"He's a sign, Linx. This baby is a sign that I'm on the right path. That what I'm doing with my life is perfect and correct."

Linx pushes himself onto the counter and hits his head on

one of the cupboards. He rubs his skull and frowns. "That doesn't make any sense to me. What sign? You stole a newborn lamb from its mother, from a flock of sheep wandering around downtown Boise. The whole situation was odd and then you had to go and kidnap a baby animal. There were cops everywhere. What if they find you and ticket you or something?"

The milk in the cup is almost gone and she'll have to heat more. The lamb is stirring, kicking out his legs. One of his ears flicks about, doing little turns and twists.

"I left the ewe the female. I took the male. It makes sense," she says and then stops herself from saying anymore. She knows that it *doesn't* make sense, not to Linx. And the more she says sends her further down the hole she's digging, making her sound crazier. The last thing Peach wants is for Linx to think she's crazy. He's her best friend and a true companion. He's perhaps the only person who will accept her once she undergoes the change that's coming. At least she hopes.

Linx slips down from the counter and takes the glass from Peach's hand. He pours more of the rich colostrum into the container and nukes it. "Thirty seconds?" he asks.

She nods, her eyes growing teary. The ram truly is a gift and for all her odd actions and nonsensical rants, Linx has already given up his protests to help Peach.

The first sound the ram makes is a weak bleat. Then he pushes himself up, hinging at his knees, and stands on the second-hand quilt. Peach reaches her arms around the lamb in case he wobbles and falls. She wants to protect him from the sharp angles of the wooden cabinets and the base of her stainless steel refrigerator.

She feels bolder than ever. More resolute. Peach has brought a bit of the sacred, the holy into her life and she knows it's just the beginning. The ram tips slightly, his drying wool grazing her fingers, but regains his balance and bleats again, louder. Then two more bleats. Five more.

"He's going to be so strong," Peach cries. Linx passes her the glass of warm milk and then resumes his roost on the counter, watching the show through narrowed eyes.

SUMMER, 1999

47 RILEY

His father puts his finger on the title of each class elective as he reads them aloud to Riley.

"See, Pre-Law," he says and pokes at the word. "They offer it as a high school elective. I'm sure it's the basics of our judicial system taught in simple terms but it won't hurt as a primer before college. Put it down as a first choice with French 4 as a second choice."

Riley hates law and the French language, but he finds himself writing out each of the course titles in caps, putting each letter into the separate boxes printed lightly on his registration form. He wonders why the French can't spell their words phonetically. He can't get behind a language that disregards all the consonants and extra vowels they put on the ends of their words without pronouncing them.

"Dad, they say 'calm' like we do, but they spell it c-a-l-m-e-s."

His father unknots his tie and slips out of a navy sports

jacket. He ignores Riley's bit of trivia. "If we don't start you off with the foundations for pre-law in college, we have less of a legacy to show law schools when you graduate. It's all about showing them you're serious from the get go, as early as high school."

High school graduation is years away, then another four years of college, and Riley gives in to the fact his father has his next eight years of life already micromanaged. And if his dad gets his wish, if the colleges note the effect of his father's interest in law, he can expect an additional three years of academia. Part of him wants to start a fight with the tall man with broad shoulders who insists on wearing a tie, even on weekends. But he figures if he does what his father wants, he can smuggle in a few of his own dreams, too. His father might support them if he falls in line.

"But track is still on, right?" he asks his dad, completing his form. "I get to keep running?"

His dad hands him the list of classes and nods. "If you keep your grades up, I don't mind if you run the rest of your life. It builds character and discipline. You'll need it to succeed in the world of litigation."

Riley sticks a flat piece of Juicy Fruit in his mouth and squeezes the gum against his teeth. He's okay with potentially hating his day job when he's forty. At least he'll have money, nice cars, maybe even a hot wife. He's okay with the fact his father has decided to make his career choice for him. His father's a smart man, maybe even a genius, and Riley trusts his judgment.

Besides, Riley may end up being an indifferent lawyer, but he knows what he loves. The feel of asphalt smacking the soles of his shoes when his heel hits the ground, the smell of a girl when she hasn't showered for a day, the admiration, even jealousy of other guys when Riley shows the world how awesome he really is.

"Top of the pile," he says out loud to his dad who responds by handing him a twenty. He promises Riley more money when he brings home an A in his Pre-Law class this coming fall.

"I hope you never chew gum in class," his father says before picking up a magazine on Civil War miniatures. His father paints the tiny, metal figures in tones of blue and gray with dollops of red on weekend evenings at home.

"Never have," he says, thinks about the last time he was caught chewing gum and sticking it to Ms. Jarret's dry erase board. Each time he did it, he made sure he was found out. Each time he spent an hour in detention with her, alone, watching her grade papers at her desk, the opening of her blazer and her V-neck sweaters enough to keep his mind off lawyers and lawsuits and the satisfaction of his father.

SUMMER, 2014

48 PEACH

Though the heat of the summer turns her car into a furnace, she refuses to roll down the windows of her Honda and let a bit of air in. She shivers, despite the warmth, and pops a stick of gum into her mouth to give her body something else to do aside from sending goosebumps up her forearms. Her car is stationary in the parking lot of a strip club she's only ever driven by and frowned at with open disgust. Now she considers going inside the building and having a look around. If she's done her research correctly, there might be someone inside who could be of interest and importance to her in several significant ways.

But she never touches the handle of the door and chews her gum until all the flavor of spearmint has dissolved down her throat and she's left with a bit of rubbery matter mashed between her tongue and hard palate. She looks around the asphalt pavement littered with detritus, afraid someone will see her sitting alone in the car in the middle of the day. She wonders if she knows anyone who comes to the club and if they'll find her in the parking lot. She has no story to tell them of why she's there. She'll likely just turn over the engine if anyone comes inquiring, speed away without giving them an answer.

"You can do this," she pep talks herself. She turns on her engine and flips on the A/C but with the car in park, all she gets is stale, hot air. "You've got to get over what people might think of you, Peach. You don't need to explain yourself to anyone. No one could understand, anyway."

A woman walks out of the club. She wears cutoffs and a skimpy tank top. A man has his arm slung around her shoulders. He's taller than the woman by a head and they turn in toward one another as they walk to a late-model sedan. When they get to the vehicle, the man fishes for keys while the woman leans her body against the metal of the car. Peach can hear her yelp as the flesh on her hamstrings gets scorched. She rubs at her legs and pouts for the man, her lips spread open, ruby like the flayed open belly of a newly-caught salmon.

Peach slides down a bit in her seat, hoping the couple doesn't see her. They don't know her, but she wants to stay invisible regardless. She reaches her arm over to the passenger side of the Honda and pulls a small notebook out from under the seat. Its cover is teal; a pen is attached to the binding via its cap.

Flipping open the Moleskine book, she thumbs through the pages and looks down to what's written and drawn there. Then she looks back up at the woman who now reaches her arms up to curve them around the man's neck. He puts his hands on her ass and lifts her off the ground, her feet dangling, dragged down by a heavy set of wedges strapped across her toes.

It might be her, is probably her, but she doesn't want to be too cocky in her sense of surety. If it is her, she marvels at the odds of such a tangled connection. Peach needs to be dead on about this woman, has to check her research with a face-to-face encounter. But not today. She watches the man and woman get in the car after a minute of desperate groping in the parking lot and drive away. She keeps her position in her car, miniature notebook open in her lap until she can unfreeze her body and put her hands on the wheel.

"Next time I'll at least get out of the car," she speaks to herself. "After that I might go inside. Little steps. Baby steps. I have time yet to make my first move."

WEDNESDAY, THE 8TH OF APRIL, 2015

49   RILEY

It's the same man with the bulging eyes partially
responsible for his injury, his coworker named Newt, who asks
Riley if he can do a pirouette when he limps into High Desert
Trommel. The man demonstrates a spin, pitching up on one of
his feet, his toes spinning on the short carpeting of the shop's
showroom floor. Riley knows the accident was more his fault
than anyone else's, but the man teasing him was also to blame.
And instead of some remorse, sympathy or an apology, he
dances, his arms flinging out in wide circles, to the snickers and
guffaws of the other metal workers.

"That one was a bit of modern dance," Newt informs and
Riley looks away to a shelf of collapsible shovels.

"All right, boys," Double Al tucks his shirt in at his waist,
the tail coming untucked at the small of his back. His sizable
middle is covered in green flannel and a tape measure is clipped
to his belt. "Any of you could be in an accident here. Didn't your
mothers teach you any better?"

185

Riley had been proud of himself. He'd been able to leave his crutches in his Nissan and make his way slowly to the shop nestled between a furniture maker and an airplane hangar on the outskirts of West Boise. His day had begun well, and he thought he'd show off some of his resilience and fortitude with the visit to his workplace. But his coworkers were in their usual mood to mock him. Sometimes Riley felt as though the business was less about work and more about hierarchy and bullshit to these men. He felt like he was back in junior high school, except this time he wasn't popular. And he needed another grown man to defend his honor.

"Did you keep them?" another of his coworkers asks. This man runs the front office when he's not bending metal in the backroom. "Put them on a string or in a jar? It'd be sort of badass like *Lord of the Flies*."

"Except I didn't cut off my own toes or anyone else's toes. I didn't go on some homicidal, primal rage in the depths of a humid, island jungle absent adults. Also, I don't think William Golding would refer to *Lord of the Flies* as badass. So no, it's really nothing like that," Riley says.

"Who is William Golding?" asks a different coworker with a smear of grease on one of his cheekbones.

Double Al puts a hand on Riley's shoulder and presses him toward his office. Riley leads the way slowly, focused on putting his weight on his left heel when he steps and holding his chest high and forward. When Double Al closes the door behind them, he lets his confidence crumble just a bit and slips into a torn leather chair patched with silver duct tape.

"You wouldn't have believed the crap they gave me when I started this business, son," Double Al says and remains standing. He pops open a glass canister of cinnamon bears and offers them to Riley after tossing a few in his own mouth. "A man, a black man, who knew nothing of mining but wanted to make machines to turn soil and find gold? And in Idaho? Hell, getting good fabricators and blacksmiths in here took a solid six months."

Riley waves away the candy and rubs at the knee on his left leg, achy from the tension of holding his foot just so.

"What I'm saying is they'll all calm down about your past as a lawyer someday. Half of them never got to college. It's jealousy, Riley, and you'd be good to just let it be."

"I just wanted to stop and show everyone I was healing," Riley explains, "not get a load of shit from them."

The smell of cinnamon permeates the office and Double Al picks at a piece of red gummy stuck between his teeth. He changes the subject abruptly.

"I've been chatting with our insurance agent. Things should be okay for your medical bills. Especially since I said it wasn't your fault."

"Okay," Riley hesitates, "but it was. I didn't check the chain well enough."

The candy jar is opened again, three more soft bears placed in Double Al's mouth. He talks as he chews. "Son, as long as we corroborate, we're golden. Faulty equipment. Something. You just follow my lead. Last thing you need is missing toes and thousands of dollars of debt."

And like that, Double Al switches focus again, putting his hand up when Riley tries to speak.

"And I'm taking you to dinner on Friday night. Cancel your other plans to eat takeout and watch a soccer game."

"I hate soccer," Riley says and thinks of his plans for the coming Friday. They likely included a trip to Blaze Lounge.

But Double Al watches his face and chews away at his sweets. Double Al's eyes close slightly, making him look even more amiable and understanding. Riley suddenly doesn't want to let down his boss. Even if the meal will be an onslaught of reasons why Riley needs to come back to work, it's the least he can do for the man who's willing to lie a bit to make sure the accident insurance claim passes muster.

"And I'm not saying I'm coming back to my job," Riley continues, "but I could definitely do with a dinner out."

Double Al plucks one more cinnamon bear from the jar and walks to Riley. He drops it into Riley's lap and smiles.

"Great, son. Eat a bear. With me, it's always dessert first."

50   PEACH

She thought she would never come to this place on a lunch break. But with the incident of the sheep downtown and the lamb sequestered at home in her bedroom, Peach is feeling daring and ready to push herself harder toward her goal. Besides, her time to act is growing shorter.

Sev is at his usual spot, perched on a high stool at the bar. He holds a pen in his left hand and a glass of gin and tonic in his right. His puffy cheeks cinch back into a smile when he sees Peach. She waves politely at him and makes to walk to her usual table in the back of the room, but Sev motions her over and pats the cushioned foam of the stool next to his.

Peach checks the stage for Nell. She's there, dancing to a nearly empty building. She doesn't notice Peach's entrance. In her purse are two twenties. Peach doesn't usually give Nell money when she finishes a dance, but she wonders if that's a mistake. It's a difficult game. She doesn't know if giving the stripper money will be normal, even flattering, or if it will seem disingenuous or insulting coming from her. Along with the daring comes the self-doubt and she's annoyed they are such tight partners.

"Don't you have a job?" Sev asks and pours Peach a glass of tepid water from a pitcher on the bar. A lemon slice bobs around in the carafe as he sets it back down.

Peach could ask him the same thing but doesn't. She looks at the napkins arrayed in front of him and takes in the poems written on each one. They're typically a few lines long. The common themes are heartache, money and blunt-force trauma. She likes the way he writes; his penmanship is strong and squat and he inks like his words need to be as black as a night without moonlight.

Sev lifts his glass and they clink bottoms. Peach takes a sip of water and it takes slightly of dishwashing liquid. "So, your girlfriend," she begins, "is a talented dancer."

"It's not her, though," Sev answers, his pen pressed down on a new, white napkin. "She's going to be a dental hygienist and stop flashing her norks around. She could be an accountant or mathematician. She happens to be a bit of a savant with numbers, except she hates math. And I'm here to make sure she doesn't stay around for more than the money. Keep her safe, you know. Keep her focused on her future. And I'm a bit of a dick with the men. The owner doesn't mind as long as I don't overstep. He understands tough love."

Peach watches Nell bend forward. She's topless, but her nipples are capped in flesh-colored pasties. The sight makes Peach shift uncomfortably in her seat.

"But is she a trained dancer? She looks so light."

"Not as small as you, enchantress," Sev says, appraising Peach's body. "She's not a ballerina or anything. But she's fit, healthy. Could deck a prick if need be."

The front door opens and sun along with a blast of fresh air hits Peach's face. She breathes it quickly in before the door shuts and they're enveloped by dark and neon once more. She wonders how strong Nell is, how her body would feel pressed up against her own.

"You like my girl?" Sev asks and then winks. One of his earrings jangles when he tilts his head at Peach. "I don't mind girls liking my Nell. That's different. Sapphic, even. You know, enchantress, you're more transparent than you think."

Peach is speechless and not just metaphorically. She tries to talk and no sound issues from her throat. The poet's instincts are right. But she wishes, pleads with the stars hidden overhead—the ceiling and the power of sunlight keeping them from her—that she's not too transparent.

"And if you like a bit of cock with your ladies," Sev goes on, his fingertips brushing one of Peach's knees, "then we can make something work."

She shuffles off her stool, nearly twisting her ankle when she hits the floor. She does her best not to look out of sorts or embarrassed. She tosses her purse on the bar top and smiles at the man she thinks of as a giant, aggressive snake.

"Excuse me. I've got to hit the bathroom."

And to solidify her self-assurance, to make it seem as though she is calm and secure, she leaves her bag on the bar with Sev. As she retreats to the washroom, she passes through the nearly empty room. Just outside the hallway leading to the restrooms, a man sits alone in a chair not far from the table she typically frequents. He's older, perhaps in his fifties or sixties, with skin the color of stained wood and a braid of flawless white hair running down his neck. When she passes him, he lifts his index finger and shakes it at her. It's a motion half-wave, half-admonishment and she looks again briefly at the man and finds him suave and sexually stunning. She has the sharp feeling in her gut of wanting his finger to beckon, not reprimand, but she nudges away the desire for the man and enters the ladies restroom.

191

She locks the door and takes in the space. There's one toilet without a stall and a small cabinet to the side of a freestanding sink. A plug-in freshener has the room smelling of syrupy, artificial mango and a decal over the mirror reminds all employees and patrons to wash their hands.

Gripping the sides of the sink, Peach talks to herself, tells herself Sev is correct about a few things, and first among them is her enchanting nature. Peach repeats the name over and over in her mind, willing it to be true. Enchantress. She forces herself to believe it; she feels more engaging, charming and attractive. She imagines shape shifting into the man sitting at the table she just passed, full to bursting with sensual energy and confidence. These are traits she must possess if she plans on becoming what Michel would call Perfect Peach. She thinks then of her client with the lacy eyelashes and solitary cigarette, with his misplaced amour toward Peach and smiles to the mirror over the sink.

She got him, even though his admiration is wildly inappropriate. She can get others.

The skin on her scalp comes to life, as if a hundred black ants are meandering about under her wig. She slips a hand under the hair and tickles away the itch in the same spot as always, the place where neck meets skull.

"Focus," she says out loud to the mirror and then looks over at the door, making sure it's locked. "You can do this. You can get Nell away from him. You're running out of time, Peach. Use your skills. You're the enchantress."

Suddenly the itch that was subdued by her fingers becomes a sharp pain and shots of agony lace her neck, back and forehead. She hasn't had a migraine in some time, but the signs are there, unforgettable from her college years and adolescence when she frequently felt their debilitating effects.

Except this time there's something different. Her peripheral vision contracts in both eyes, until the bathroom grows dark and she stands, blinded, clutching the sink. A second later, bursts of jagged flame and white zips of lightning explode into her field of vision. She watches the lights tremble and dance, a display of fire, until her sight recovers, an aperture opening once again to let in the shadows which slowly transform into the pedestal sink, toilet, peeling wallpaper.

"That's next," she says, her hands placed at the nape of her neck and forehead, trying to press away the pounding in her head. "Of course. Thank you."

51   RILEY

On his way back home from visiting his workplace, Riley
spots a transient at the corner of one of the approaching
intersections. He says a little prayer to God or that bitch, life,
that he won't be the one to stop next to the man, that the light
will turn green and he won't be left idling in his Nissan, doing
his best to avoid the stares of the weak and forgotten.

But this is exactly what does happen. Riley stares ahead, his
hands firmly on the steering wheel. The timing on the light
seems interminably long; the intersection is a busy one with four
lanes of traffic converging from the cardinal directions.

And though he doesn't really want to, he forces himself to
turn his head and take in the man on the corner. He wears a
brown trench coat, mud at its hem and a faux fur hat that looks
like it came out of Russia or some other Slavic nation. He has a
small wooden trailer attached to a mountain bike that was likely
made in the eighties, its frame thick and unwieldy. He holds up a
sign made from a flattened moving box. The letters are bold,

written in dark blue marker:

*Life's gotten me. I'm showing my underbelly. Care to help
me up?*

Riley thinks of the way Harlequin, his chocolate lab, would
flip onto her back and wriggle when she'd tipped over the trash
or snatched a bit of food from the dining table. And he knows
this man feels like he's doing his best to show he's vulnerable,
that if life wants, life can tear open his throat and leave him to
bleed out.

It's an image Riley confronts as well on the silent nights,
when the whisky and the OxyContin won't quiet his foot or his
mind. The thought was there before the accident, too. He feels
he's been submissive to the whims of a harsh mistress, to life, for
over a year now. And now he just wants to get up, reclaim his
feet and peel back his lips in a snarl.

The light turns green, but instead of moving, Riley rolls
down his passenger window and the homeless man walks over, a
discernable shamble in his step. Riley pulls open his glove
compartment and roots around for a ten-dollar bill he keeps
under his vehicle manual. The drivers behind him protest by
honking. Someone lays a hand against their horn and leaves it
there.

The bill is found and Riley shoves it at the man. But the
homeless man misses it and the wind catches it, holds it on a
wisp of air, and then spins it away from his hands. He shouts his
thanks as he shuffles away after the bill, aloft like a green leaf
first to fall in autumn.

Riley presses on the gas, gains speed and leaves the other
drivers car lengths behind him. He needs to make a choice if he
doesn't want to be the man chasing potential as it flies away
from him. It's time for him to buck up, toughen up, make his
dead father and his employer proud.

"I'm going back to work," he says to the rearview mirror.
"Fuck you, life."

THURSDAY,
THE 9TH OF APRIL,
2015

52   PEACH

She'd promised Linx sex. It was what she had to do to get him to watch the lamb for the evening while she took I-84 west out of Boise. Nothing else had placated him, but when she alluded to getting physical when she got back to the apartment after the drive, he stopped pressing to know where she was headed and went into the kitchen to heat up milk for the lamb. She was using raw goat's milk now on the baby, mixing it with the small amount of colostrum-laden milk she had left in the fridge.

Peach experiences one of her least favorite things about driving west: driving into the garish flare of the setting sun. Its orange-red glare isn't deflected by the visor and she forgot sunglasses. She keeps one hand on the wheel and the other, fingers tight, against her forehead to fight the light. When she sees the off-ramp to Parma, she takes it and then pulls a sharp right, parks her car in a gravel lot.

The building is yellow and white and a large, plastic tarp

pinned to the understory of the roof advertizes two things: fireworks and furs.

Inside, she's greeted with an abundance of both. The smell of gunpowder and tanned leather fight for dominance in her nose and she stops before looking at anything closely, spinning slightly to take in the heads of deer, fox, and ermine mounted high along the walls of the concrete block store. She runs her fingers between a pile of small, dark furs of indeterminate origin. The sign merely advertizes them as *fifteen a piece* but she doesn't know which animal's life is considered so cheap.

She thinks of her lamb at home, how he stands and walks solidly now, how she takes him out at night to roll in the grass of the common area and nuzzle his face in the dirt. Horns catch her eye and she can see a head of a bighorn sheep mounted near a display case of mortars. It must have been a magnificent ram when it hopped the rocks of some mountainous stronghold. Its real, previously-operable eyes have been replaced with black glass. But the two thick, tan horns which curl over twice upon themselves are the real thing.

Peach wanders toward the stacks of ground blooms, tables laden with fountains and hollow cardboard tubes meant to shoot mortars of chemical powder and ground metal into the sky. She fingers some of the fireworks, turns over their packaging. The instructions are written in nonsensical English. A box of sparklers promises to *okay fire from stick tops.*

Moving past the illegal explosives, Peach finds an area with cones, mid-sized fountains and a few giant boxes pushed to the center of the flammable display. She picks through them, looking for fireworks with specific characteristics: red sparks, globular flame that looks like lava, ones that make no sound. And then from all she finds she culls to a handful with names that speak to her: Volcano Eruption, Fire of Olympus, Flames 5X and Maximum Magma. At least the Chinese get someone creative with decent English vocabulary to come up with the monikers if not the firework descriptions.

A mustached man in a denim vest wanders over to Peach and tips his head at the small arsenal piled on the table in front of her.

"Not going to have much of a celebration without a finale piece. Let me show you one like these but longer. It'll shoot red and white into the sky for a full minute."

"Let's take a look," she says, tucks her cache into a basket the man pulls from underneath the table. "I'm sold if it's got a good name and no whistles or loud booms."

"Souls of Hades," he says, not missing a beat. Peach figures he knows every firework in the store by name.

"That will likely work," she says and follows him between the rows of contained power waiting to be set alight and the preserved hides of dead animals ready to be engulfed in flame and put to rest if the opportunity ever allows.

FRIDAY, THE 10TH OF APRIL, 2015

53   RILEY

The old Dodge Ram drives in the direction of downtown, but Double Al refuses to tell Riley where they're going to dinner. He insists on it being a surprise and Riley lets his boss have his fun. The wheels run over one of the red symbols, one of the strange Vs still painted at the intersection of Broadway and Front. The color is starting to fade and Riley wonders out loud when they'll get around to cleaning the graffiti off the asphalt.

"They're still all around the city," Double Al says, "and they haven't hurt anyone yet. Just a deviant messing around, I suspect."

When they get close to the city center, Double Al hangs a left on a one-way street near the Connector that runs a circuit through the city and out to the interstate. He pulls his truck alongside a sidewalk and throws it in park. He tells Riley to hold on and then he jumps down from the truck cab to the sidewalk, passing a row of fragrant junipers as he moves around to Riley's door.

Riley looks around to see whom might be watching the coming scene, slightly embarrassed about being helped out of the vehicle by an overweight man with more decades behind him than in front of him. But he lets his boss take him by the forearms until his feet are safely on the ground.

"See, no need for physical therapy," he says to Double Al. The man responds with a sigh and a stretching of his fingertips tight against one another to pop his knuckles.

Double Al doesn't bother to lock up the truck and tugs up on his pants. He's dressed in jeans, as usual, but he wears a nice sweater and a shirt with a collar underneath it.

"Someone wants the old thing, they can take her."

Then he switches topics, true to form. "You okay with walking just a bit. I've never been to this place, but I don't think it's far off."

"I'm good," Riley says and takes a tentative step after exiting his seat in the truck. He's sans crutches again. He feels strong tonight and after he puts his feet down a few times, he relaxes into the cadence of his slightly unbalanced steps.

They walk a few blocks, moving further into downtown. Riley lets himself enjoy the early evening, the air still a bit warm from the setting sun and the concrete releasing the pent up heat of the day, no matter how fleeting and weak. They pass groups of people out enjoying the longer days and the beginning of the weekend. He catches snippets of birdsong: an orchestra of sparrow twitters and the deeper caws of crows.

Riley thinks back to last weekend and the strange scene of the barricades and the sheep. He hasn't said anything to Double Al about being downtown during the fiasco which ended up making national news. Nor has he mentioned Hamal to anyone but Walker. He doesn't want to bring any of it up now, his thoughts about the letters or his thoughts about his role in society, as a man, and ruin the dinner they stroll toward.

A trio of women are coming from the opposite direction of

the men, and Double Al stops a bit short to move behind Riley and share the sidewalk with the other pedestrians. Riley sees her then. She's still slight, her small torso enveloped in an oversized cardigan. Her brown hair is pulled back into a ponytail and she chats quickly and loudly with her walking companions.

He does his best to move like he used to when he had ten toes instead of five, with a clean stride, his chin high and his eyes looking ahead. But the newness of his wounded foot keeps him slow and ungainly.

They pass the women and the one he notices takes notice of him, turning her head just in time to murmur a quiet hello. He lifts his fingers in recognition, never bringing them higher than his hip. She leaves him with the scent of her tuberose perfume.

Double Al takes back up his position at Riley's side and nudges him in the ribs with an elbow.

"She was a cute one, son. How you know her?"

"She's a girl I used to screw. Her name's Nicole," he says and fights the desire to crane his neck around and get a look at her walking away.

Double Al keeps at him. "So what went wrong?"

"Nothing," Riley says.

He's feeling better with each step away from the woman. He thinks if he's really lucky and Life—the uppercase L kind with its grudge against Riley—gets back on his side, he might be able to run again someday. He's sure of it. With the Hacky Sac in his shoe and a completely healed stub of a foot, he'll be a gazelle once again.

"She couldn't stop being my girlfriend's best friend. So that put a damper on things."

Double Al laughs so loudly he draws the attention of another approaching group of revelers. They flash grins in response to his merriment. There is an underlying wheeze to Double Al's chuckling and the man stops for a moment to cough up something into a handkerchief that has seen hundreds of washes over the years. He wipes at his lips and then unveils the smile still plastered there.

"Good thing that anvil landed on your toes, son. Could have taken out something else on your body you use a lot more."

"Thankfully women don't think much of a man's toes," Riley quips.

His stride smoothes out once the pressure to perform disappears. Channeling a gazelle may be a possibility much sooner than he predicted. He can imagine the sandy soil of the Serengeti under his feet, his muscles warm from giving some massive feline the slip, the pupils of his eyes deep black and shiny with life.

54   PEACH

It's her third outing with the dark green duffel bag. The first was the night she went out for a "run." The second was the evening before the flock of sheep invaded the Basque Block. She is beginning to get used to the feel of the textured straps in her palm. But the weight of the thing is always changing, depending on its contents. And this evening, as she wanders around downtown, the bag is light and easy to carry.

Peach is a planner and she knows what her movements and actions are about well before setting her intentions into motion. So tonight she feels mentally foggy, because instead of her head being in charge, it's her gut. Or rather it's the center of power just below her belly button. She had found herself compelled to head downtown, to ask Linx once again to watch the lamb, knowing she would have to placate him with promises of intimacy, perhaps even a solid night together in the same bed. She hopes her instincts are right to see her wandering the streets with the contents of the bag, her torso covered in her well-worn, dark woolen hoodie. She has no idea what it is she needs to look for or where she will end up. For now, she feels intrepid, an adventurer on home soil, and reminds herself this is what she wants to be. So she lets it be and keeps moving.

The sun hides behind a tall bank building and Peach drifts about in the dusky dim of the night, absently letting her feet choose where she treads. She avoids people, has a desirous craving for a cup of coffee but talks herself out of going into a restaurant or a café.

And then she sees a thing of such beauty and opportunity she shakes her head at the sight of it. She almost misses it, keeping her head down and watching the indents in the sidewalk slip by as she racks up footfalls. But she looks up just in time to take in the sparkle of gold to her right.

Hanging from the rearview mirror of a gray Dodge Ram decades old and well-used, is a chunky bit of what looks to be gold. She stops briefly and presses her face to the window causing the plane of glass to fog over with her breath. What appears to be gold is really fool's gold, iron pyrite. And this is what makes her shake her head. This piece of metal dangling inside the old truck is a thing of righteous and rare luck.

She knows seeing this particular truck with this particular piece of metal hanging inside of it is not a play of coincidence. It is fate, meaningful in its synchronicity. Peach does not believe in coincidence anyway. Her world is one of omens and relationships, energy and connections. Causes will always have effects, but those two things can be separated by vast amounts of time and space.

Peach looks up to the pale blue of the sky. The sun will be put to bed soon and the stars will do their best to shine through the smog and the lit windows of the little city surrounding her. It's no matter, really. She can speak to the stars without seeing them. She directs her whisper to Mars as well, spinning its red body around in the heavens unseen.

"I trust and I am rewarded. I am led and so I follow. Thank
you. All of you."

She sets down her duffel bag on the sidewalk and looks up
and down the street to see how secluded she is. There are groups
of people wandering around and she realizes she'll have to be
patient. But she won't let the opportunity escape her. She runs
her gloved hands along the side of the truck. It's remarkably well
preserved for its age, absent of large dents and long scratches.

She sees the growth of the junipers in their pocket of earth
against the length of the sidewalk and she paces next to them
until a scraggly bush with only one branch flush with green, the
others bare, white bark flaking, creates a gap for her to swing a
leg over the hedge. She hunches down behind the bushes and
takes in their sharp, pungent scent and slips her hood over her
head, knotting the drawstrings at her throat. Her wig shifts
slightly and that itch is back at the base of her skull.

Pulling at the bottom of her hooded sweater, she finds a
little snag in the stitching at the hem. She takes off her gloves
and picks at the thread with her fingernails until it comes away
from the rest of the wool. At the weakened seam, she grips the
fabric in her fingers and holds the hem steady with her left hand
while yanking with her right. A strip of wool comes away in her
palm. Peach holds the dyed fabric up to her face then looks down
to her ruined sweater.

Then she strips away another swatch and another, until her
sweater is a midriff thing, riding high, just above her belly
button, uncovering the pulsing, radiating point of energy hidden
away inside of her.

55 RILEY

"You could have bought me a corsage," Riley jokes. "I feel like we're on a date."

The waiter sets two rib eye steaks in front of the men and asks if they need anything else before backing away. The restaurant is the nicest steakhouse in Boise. The tables are covered in white linens and tea lights illuminate the cozy, dark ambiance with a subtle glow.

Double Al smiles and Riley can tell he's in the rare mood to play along with his jests. "I didn't know what you were going to wear. I was worried orchids wouldn't match. And then I'd be kicking myself about not getting something simple like carnations."

"So I'm impressed," Riley says, slicing into his meat. A trickle of blood seeps out of the rare cut. "Because you want me to be impressed. So I'll come back to work, right?"

"Something like that," the man says and picks the parsley garnish off his plate and sets it to the side of his salad fork.

"I've been wondering why you think I won't come back to work, Double Al. As if a bit of amputation will keep me away?" Riley puts on a good show of making it seem he never considered staying in his pajamas for the next five years.

"I've seen others get hurt. And when they do, that fear about work, and then a fear of life gets in them and starts to take over. They become paralyzed and unable to do more than drink on a sofa all day."

Riley thinks of his fondness for whisky. He picks up the glass of tawny liquid in front of him now, smells its sweet bite before taking a sip. He agrees with Double Al more than he'd like to admit, but he also believes his downward slide came long before his toes getting smashed.

"When your dad died, your mom, too, I promised myself that I would check in on you. And after your finances," Double Al pauses, looking for the right wording, "dwindled, I thought a new line of work would do you some good. I didn't just put you in my shop because your dad and I were friends. I thought making something powerful and crafted with your own hands could do you some good. I still think it to be true."

Riley can remember Double Al's visits to their home and the presents he would bring of interesting or beautiful rocks. The man would give Riley agates, granite, pale jaspers and quartz crystals. They all came from his mining sites in the Owyhees and the Boise Basin and from his explorations near the base of the Sawtooths. Riley doesn't know what happened to all the rocks. For years he kept them tucked in a white sock yellowed with age, its partner long since missing. He'd take them out of the sock often, run their jagged or smooth weight over his fingers. He thinks he even gave them names at one point. Now, they were lost to him.

"It did do me good. I did pick up some of the pieces of my life when you hired me on. But I don't know," Riley looks at Double Al tucking into a spread of red potatoes, "it's not my dream to make mining equipment. I'm not even sure I have a dream. Other than to become a man again."

Double Al wipes at his mouth with a fabric napkin and frowns. "What does that mean, son? Become a man again? You are one. Just need to believe it and live it."

A swig of alcohol burns its way down Riley's throat. He can see the image of Nell in front of him, the swing of her hips and the way she can vibrate the muscles in her ass. "I'm starting to believe it again," he says.

56   PEACH

With the sun finally gone, the street turns quiet and empties
of other souls. Peach opens her duffel bag and lines up the
cardboard boxes and cones on the edge of the sidewalk. Using a
long-handled lighter, she ignites each fuse on the fireworks and
backs away. They spit skyward: displays of silver crackles,
golden drops of fire and red blobs of liquefied metal. All of them
are silent excepting the pop of new powder chambers catching
fire and a low hiss of the heat escaping the confines of the
fireworks, the chemical reactions within a thing of spectacular
power.

"You did it," she tells herself as she zips up her bag and
looks around her, doing what's necessary to clean up her space.
She can't leave a trace of herself behind. Not even a trace of Old
Peach. The slight hiss of the pyrotechnics is background music
to her tidying.

She smiles to herself and whispers. "It's a wonderful
gesture. There is no doubt. Fire for Fire!"

It's not long before flames and minute flecks of burning chemical compounds lick the wool strips she's placed strategically. The material singes at the edges first, the thick fabric smoldering like the embers of a campfire. Peach looks up at the stars and grins, blows them all a giant kiss with her fingers flinging high to the firmament.

There had been no control on her part. She'd come downtown with her purchases and then trusted she'd receive guidance. Peach feels the reward of having faith, of paying respect to those powers more awesome and awful than she. Her work here is finished. What the event will contribute to her change, she cannot guess at.

One more kiss from her lips and then she runs. She hates running. But she'll run when she must, when she has all the right reasons to make herself fly.

57 RILEY

The men have moved on to brownies coated in rich fudge sauce. Riley licks the black stickiness from the back of his spoon and can feel the grit of sugar on his teeth.

Riley has played hard to get the entire meal at the nice steakhouse with Double Al. He's nearly done finishing up on his diatribe of all the reasons he'd be a bad fit back on the machine shop floor. "My balance is horrible with my toes gone. Not sure I could plant myself well enough to swing a sledge."

Double Al pushes his plate away. "You can work the front office for awhile. Just until you feel ready to get back in the shop. Talk to customers and do a little paper pushing. Maybe you can help me update my files and get them all on a computer. Newt told me it wasn't 1991 anymore."

"Newt's a choad. I'd be your assistant?" Riley asks. He's okay with the idea. It would be good to do some desk work, keep himself busy until he can get back in to bending metal.

"You'd be whatever you want. It's work, son. You need it."

And then the restaurant is enveloped in a deafening boom.

Nothing physically is damaged; the only thing which moves is the small tea light on their table, inching a bit to the right. But the patrons of the steakhouse cover their mouths, some stand up from tables, napkins stuck to their pants. A baby screams out then its voice slides into sobs of terror.

"What the hell?" Riley says, unable to keep his seat either. Double Al scoots out his chair and the two of them, along with half of the restaurant, funnel outside to see what's happening.

A whirl of black smoke billows into the sky, hard to see with the arrival of night. But the white tinges of smoke in the dark funnel shimmer under the lights of the businesses still open during the evening. Double Al sets out for the explosion a few blocks away, Riley doing his best to keep up with him.

"Near the truck," is all the man says as he picks up walking speed.

They cover the few blocks to the Dodge Ram in a minute or two, Riley's foot pleading for him to ease up on the speed with sharp jabs to his shin bone. But he ignores the pain, as anxious as Double Al to make sure the truck is okay.

A small group of people stand a half block away from where the men parked the vehicle, cell phones out, recording the monstrous flame. And then Riley can see the explosion isn't near the truck. It *is* the truck. The '93 Dodge Ram is a mess of smoking metal and burning tires. The acrid zip of combusting rubber settles in the still air. The junipers near the truck are fat candles of fire, their branches intertwined with one another, trading the blaze from bush to bush as if they pass a dish of Bananas Foster.

Sirens fill the night and Double Al rubs at his eyes, disbelief and confusion overwhelming him.

"How?" is all he says. "How?"

Riley can see the inside of the truck, the upholstery fuel for the flames. The iron pyrite still dangles from the mirror, its metal sides reflecting the burn. Then the small line of string holding it aloft combusts and the fool's gold falls into the fire busy melting the gearshift.

Riley's emotions and thoughts are as explosive and consuming as the fire in front of him. He'd been so sure about going back to work and falling in line with what was expected of him. Now, as he watches something so solid turning to ash, he wavers in his resolution. He sees the fire and knows he can't defeat it with passivity and submission. It will keep burning.

His mind shifts, his perspective flip-flops and he's back to a previous notion on living life.

"I'm not going back to work," he says under his breath. "Fuck it."

58 PEACH

When she gets home, Linx is inside the dog kennel fencing Peach strung about the center of the living room. She moved the animal there from her bedroom, to contain the lamb after he gummed a hole in her comforter. He's scratching the ram behind its ears and singing gently to it in a mishmash of Thai and English the song "You Are My Sunshine." She left her torn and mangled sweater in the car along with the empty duffel bag. A shiver crawls up her arms as she listens to the song and watches the way the lamb gently butts its forehead against Linx's legs.

"I thought I was your sunshine," she says and Linx stops his performance. He looks Peach over and points at her hands.

"You had me watch Harry so you could play in soot? What's with the black fingers?"

Peach tucks her hands in the pockets of her dark cargo pants. She watches the lamb, sturdy on his legs, his nostrils snuffing out her arrival into the room. "His name isn't Harry. I'm naming him. I just haven't gotten around to it yet."

"I'll call him Harry until you think of something better."

Peach smirks. "How about Little Tuksin, since he likes you so much."

Linx steps out of the fenced area and moves in close to Peach. She can smell the animal on him, even though the heady scent of musky livestock has already permeated her apartment. He reaches into her pockets and pulls out her wrists. He turns her hands over in his hands, his darker skin supple from the lanolin produced by the lamb.

"Don't call Harry by my first name. Please. And really, what were you up to tonight?"

Peach looks down at their hands intertwined. His fingers are nearly as delicate as hers. But hers are marred by ash and the smell of gunpowder and she's suddenly thankful her apartment smells like a barnyard. It overpowers the scent of her guilt.

"I was having a night to myself. I was out having fun," she says and pulls her hands away. She heads to the bathroom and gives them a quick wash, drying them with sheets of Kleenex instead of using her light yellow towels. Linx follows her in and backs up against the doorframe.

"You seem to be having a lot of *fun* lately," Linx says, putting air quotes around the word, "but it seems to be changing you, Peach. You're getting wilder."

Peach knows what Linx means is that she's less willing to stay home and stay quiet, less willing to capitulate to his demands for a relationship. Less tame. She hopes once she makes her complete transformation, he'll still be able to pluck up her hands and hold them in his. But she's not counting on it. Not once he sees what she's become.

"I'm just pushing myself. Like we talked about a couple weeks back at the restaurant. I'm ready to be more than what I am. And I really do appreciate you supporting my desires."

Then Peach presses Linx for a bit more support and help. She's been ready to ask this of him for days, but didn't know how to broach the subject. Now is the time.

"I'm not sleeping well," she says. "I feel like I'm up all night thinking about things, worrying about life getting away from me, out of my control."

"You shouldn't be out so late," he says and by the way he nods as he speaks, Peach knows he thinks he's found her solution.

"Yes," she continues, "but your Ambien seems to work well for you, right? Maybe I need some sleeping pills. Just for awhile. So I can get some rest."

And then she seals the play with a promise of getting back to normal. "Maybe if I could sleep I wouldn't be so obsessed with this change thing. Maybe I could get back to my old self."

"Go see your doctor and get a prescription," he says, slightly intrigued by her words.

"Or you could just refill your prescription for me?" she hints. "You know I don't have good health insurance and this way I could have the pills in what, a day? I'm tired, Linx. I could really use your help with this."

Peach locks eyes with her best friend. She knows that he knows this is significant for her, the extended gaze, the purposeful connection of sight. His shoulders soften a bit and he pushes off the wall and puts his arms around her. She tries to not stiffen at his touch but relax into it. When he can feel her chest yield a bit, he squeezes harder and speaks into her hair.

"I just don't want you changing too much. I'll get you some pills."

Peach brings up her arms then and squeezes him back. Hard.

MONDAY, THE 13TH OF APRIL, 2015

59 RILEY

The officer assigned to the arson case is slim with cropped
red hair and is about ten years out from retirement. He has a lazy
eye which seems to track slowly over the papers in front of him,
a momentary click behind his good eye. Double Al shifts
uncomfortably in his chair and Riley does his best to sit still and
remain level-headed about the truck bombing. He's not sure this
Hamal person could have had something to do with the fire.
There is no indication of a connection. Until he has ample cause
to be sure, he has no desire to tell the officer about the strange
cards. For now, he's just at the station to support Double Al,
since his boss has been so considerate of him since the accident
and before, with all the opportunities he's given Riley. Besides,
Riley figures he might be of some help, having seen the Dodge
Ram on fire the other night.

Still, being in the station makes him nervous. It's not the
first time he's been in a detective's office. Earlier in his life, he'd
known where the vending machines were in the Boise Police

Department stronghold in the west of the city. His visits were memorable enough to make him crave little bags of cheese-flavored popcorn and cans of Mountain Dew during times of stress.

The cop scans the report in front of him and takes a sip of herbal tea. Riley can smell chamomile wafting up from the mug.

"You sure you don't need something to drink?" the man asks, eyes still on the paper.

Both Double Al and Riley decline the offer. The cop clears his throat and dips his teabag in the cup a few times before pitching it in a trashcan near his knees.

"So I wish I had good news for you, Mr. Loewe," the cop looks up at Double Al, "but none of the cameras in the area caught anything specific to the fire. We have zero witnesses and the fire burned so hot on account of those dry, sappy hedges nearby, that we're stuck guessing on what started the fire in the first place."

"It could have been accidental?" Riley asks, hoping it was.

The policeman nearly snorts hot liquid out his nose and dabs the liquid that does escape his mouth with his forearm. "No, that's not what I'm saying. Jesus, you think a truck can just randomly explode on its own? Without a combustible to get things cooking?"

Riley drops his chin and sighs. "Right, but I was thinking maybe like a really expertly thrown cigarette landed in a pile of spilled gasoline near the truck. Or something. Okay, when I say it out loud, it sounds stupid. No accident. Gotcha."

Double Al looks over to Riley and then the cop. His curly hair is graying at the temples and Riley swears more of the silvery color has settled over his scalp in the last few weeks. He feels sorry for his boss, his old family friend. With the accident and now a fire-bombed truck, the man has a lot to keep him busy. And Riley thinks only of shirking work and having fun. Life is short and a miserable bitch, he adds to the cliché thought.

You never know when you'll get trampled by scared sheep or incinerated in a vehicle.

"It's not just 'no accident,'" the officer says, smirk still planted on his face. "It's a matter of complexity and seriousness. It's not as easy as most people think to start a vehicle on fire. You can't just chuck a Molotov at a Lexus and get a mushroom cloud."

"We're going to be looking into who perpetrated the crime. It could have been some teenagers with M-80s. It could have been a homegrown terrorist group. Perhaps some un-medicated transient was commanded to light it up by the voice of Donald Duck booming in his head. We just don't have enough evidence to really put our teeth into a solid theory yet."

Riley crinkles his nose at the mishmash of imagery but keeps quiet.

"Detective," Double Al raises his hand like he's in a primary school classroom, "you think someone could have blown up my truck in an act of terror?"

"I'm not saying that," the officer continues, takes another sip of tea. "I'm saying that at this point, anything is possible. We have some scrapings from the sidewalk in to the lab. Something might show up there. We may get an idea on what caused the initial burn."

Riley looks again at the name placard on the man's desk. Detective Dauchaun. He doesn't care to try and pronounce the name.

"Sir," he interjects, "I know cars don't just start on fire on their own. Or shouldn't, at least. But could there have been an electrical issue or something?"

Without trying to hide his mirth, the detective begins to laugh again, this time slopping his tea on his tie. It takes him a moment to regain his composure. Riley looks over to Double Al and shrugs.

"Men, let's just say there could have been some faulty

wiring under the dash. That's completely possible. But the gas tank was wide open. That's the more likely location of the first spark."

Hamal pops into Riley's mind. In turn, the name brings to mind the cards. He hasn't assigned an imagined face and figure to the name yet. But as events surrounding Riley's life become more peculiar, he's more inclined to envision Hamal as a shadowy humanoid. One made of black smoke.

The detective leans his elbows on the desk and stares at Double Al with his good eye. His lazy eye protrudes slightly and seems to be keyed in on Riley.

"Question is, Mr. Loewe, if this wasn't done by some high school pyros or a homeless nutjob, who would want to blow up your old truck? Who hates you?"

Double Al stutters out a reply. "No one, I think. I don't know of anyone who hates me. I do my best to be right and square with everyone I meet. I take pride in my relationships and in my business dealings, detective."

Riley nods his head in agreement with his boss. He's never met a person who dislikes Double Al. His boss is a genuine guy, his actions always heartfelt and decent. But the question gets Riley thinking about the destroyed Dodge Ram.

Who hates me, Riley wonders? A whirl of names pops into his head and they come to mind so fast, they're too swift and populous to count.

TUESDAY, THE 14TH OF APRIL, 2015

60   PEACH

The Pad Thai is a little too chewy and the peanuts have gone soft in the sauce.

"So I'm not the best cook, at least not with Thai cuisine," Peach takes the last bite of her creation she can muster and uses her fork to poke at a bit of tofu on Linx's plate. "But it's meat free. Well, other than tiny shrimp. People don't love tiny shrimp as much as mammals. Vegetarian people. So you can see how much I care."

Linx sits tall, glass of iced tea in his hand. He chews his noodles carefully before swallowing and then pats his stomach in appreciation. "It's not bad for a white girl. My mom would be shocked at what you've done here, and not in a good way, but I won't call her and tell her you put way too much fish sauce in the dish."

"Is that what that is?" she says and skews up her nose. "I just thought I was smelling the lamb."

"You didn't have to cook for me. Just for getting you some

sleeping pills."

"I know," Peach says and clears away the dishes. "But you're sort of a neat guy to me."

Linx snatches her as she moves around the table and pulls her into his lap. Peach tries to keep her weight from putting too much pressure on his legs. She thinks she might have a good five or ten pounds on him.

He kisses her hard on the mouth and she doesn't return the kiss so much as lets it continue. He strips a tomato-red blazer from off her shoulders and tosses it to the kitchen floor. Her lacy bra snags on one of Linx's hangnails and he pulls away his hand with a hiss. She kisses the offended finger and then puts his hand up her skirt. He works at her gently until her body shudders and she gasps quick, tight exhalations. The noise prompts the lamb to bleat loudly, until Peach can gather herself, walk topless to the living room and shush the animal back to calm.

She moves to the bedroom and Linx follows her, watching as she leans back and lets her body fall onto the bed. She keeps her hands on her head as she falls and then shimmies toward the black headboard, smiling. Linx climbs in next to her and they fuck, hard and lovely over the white sheepskin throw.

Later, Peach decides Linx can stay the night and he pokes at her for some sort of meaning in the allowance. "So you cooked for me. We had sex and now you're actually letting me stay in your bed. I think we're in a relationship."

She picks up her copy of *The Gods of Mars* and uses it to slap Linx on the back. It's her only response and then she stands up, leaves the room and comes back with a transparent orange bottle of pills.

"They're technically yours, so do you want one?" Peach holds the bottle of Ambien out to Linx and then crawls under the sheets.

"You'd think I'd be tired after that, but I guess you just keep me awake," Linx says and runs his tongue over his teeth.

He takes a pill from the container, dodging the paperback Peach swats at him with yet again. He puts the pill in the back of his mouth and swallows.

He hands the bottle to Peach and moves a bit of hair out of her eyes. She reacts quickly, grabbing his hand and moving it down to rest on her waist. She pulls a pill, white and oblong from the bottle, and puts it on her tongue.

"My mouth is dry," she says, hopping up to walk to her master bathroom. "Need water."

Shutting the door behind her, she squats on the toilet and spreads her legs. Peach lets the pill fall from her mouth and it hits the rim of the bowl, almost zipping off across the floor. She pees and then flushes the toilet, washes her hands and strolls back to bed.

The sleeping pill goes to work quickly on Linx. He's already yawning. She picks back up her book about one of John Carter's adventures on Mars. He's a man who doesn't belong on Earth and finds a home in the stars. In this, she relates to the protagonist of the book. She reads for hours, looking over periodically to see Linx asleep, his chest raising lightly, his lips slightly parted.

61   RILEY

The three cards are heavy in his hand: a belated birthday
card, one with artwork of a sad-looking panda, the last with a
pictorial meadow of spring flowers. The bourbon in his stomach
tells him to burn the cards, to get out a book of matches, go into
his backyard, sit next to his fire pit and give the bizarre messages
to the flames. Just like Hamal may have done to Double Al's
Dodge Ram. Even if Riley sees no real correlation between the
cards and the truck. The false confidence of the alcohol makes
Riley think he can do it, too. Set fire to things. Sacrifice things.

With the cards in one hand and the bottle of Maker's Mark
in the other, he stumbles to his wallet he left on the shoe bench
in his foyer. He puts down the booze and it sloshes around in the
clear glass. Digging around in his wallet, he comes away with
the business card for Detective Dauchaun. He flips the cream-
colored rectangle printed with phone numbers and email
addresses between his fingers and then tosses it onto the
cushioned bench. It's nearly eleven at night. There are a dozen

reasons for Riley not to call the officer and share the contents of his strange cards with the man's answering machine. But none of them seem good enough to stay his hand.

Riley is mad at this Hamal and needs to tell someone other than Walker about the cards. Even if Hamal is not a firebug.

He removes his phone from his jeans and blinks, trying hard to clearly see the numbers on the keypad. He looks at the officer's primary number on the card and punches it into the phone. After seven rings, the voicemail kicks on and Riley tries to pull his thoughts into one cohesive statement. The buzz of the tone passes. His mind grinds to stillness and then he hangs up, never getting a word out.

The smell of the truck fire is so fresh in his mind Riley can call it forth at will. He tips back and lands on the bench, the tang of burning synthetics in his nose. He picks up his phone again and dials a number at random, using three of the numbers from his high school locker combination.

"Hello?" A sleepy, elderly woman answers the phone and Riley is on the cusp of finding words. His voice is tremulous.

"Who are you?" he asks.

"Who are you?" she echoes.

Riley yells into the phone. "A man! I'm a man!"

The woman yawns, then speaks. "It sounds like it, dear. You should get some sleep." Then she hangs up and Riley lets the phone fall from his hand to the hardwood floor of his foyer. He looks around his body, snatches up the three cards and throws them into the air, the cardboard folds opening slightly in the shape of Vs, faraway birds in flight, before falling to the earth, too.

SUMMER, 2003

62   PEACH

Patti tosses the bouquet of yellow yarrow and orange roses on the bedspread and then pinches the tip of her nose until it flushes maroon. Peach picks up the bouquet and twirls the stems around in her palms. She waits for the explosion.

"You're too young for marriage, Peach," she begins, the loose skin of her triceps jiggling as she shakes her arm gripping her snub nose. "You don't even know yourself. How do you think you can know another person well enough to marry them? At nineteen? Are you just doing this to spite me? You are, aren't you?"

Peach brings the flowers up to her nose and breathes deeply. The musty smell of the yarrow causes her to cough. She keeps her head bowed as she sits on the bed with one of the potential flower combinations for her wedding bouquet. This set of autumnal colors she had liked the most.

She thinks her adoptive mother might be right about her not knowing herself well enough. But she feels like marrying Adam is better than the alternative. Being alone. She's been lonely for nineteen years, surrounded by a never-ending cavalcade of new foster parents, schools, houses. She's never lacked for quantity of souls, just quality. At least Adam wants her to marry him. He's insistent, in fact. And him wanting her is better than no one wanting her at all.

And she knows one of the reasons Patti objects so adamantly to the union has nothing to do with Peach. It has to do with the fact that Patti has never been married, has never found a partner to share her life with. It must sting to see Peach engaged and planning a wedding before her twentieth birthday. But Patti doesn't bring up this fact. It's something Peach understands about Patti's perception of the world. That all events and experiences, good or bad in Peach's life, are directly related to Patti. The good ones are due to her excellent mothering. The bad ones are Peach's attempts to cause Patti suffering and disappointment.

Patti lets go of her nostrils and the rest of her face deepens in color. She fans herself with her hands and takes a sip of a tepid Diet Coke. "Is this your way of tricking me to let you move back home? Because you know how I feel about that. When you're eighteen, you're an adult and can tend to yourself. I don't respond well to manipulation, Peach. But you always try to change my rules. This marriage is just another act. Just another way of manipulating me, right?"

Peach wants to say she's been tending to herself for years, before leaving Patti's house, but she knows it's best to keep silent when Patti has her emotional tirades. Peach thinks of Adam's dark hair, the thickness of it. It might be thick enough to bend the prongs of combs. He has dark circles under his eyes, not from illness or age, but from lack of sleep combined with his Basque heritage. She doesn't care he's an older man by eleven years. What he offers her is stability, something she's never truly had in her life.

Peach bears witness as Patti, the woman who never truly wanted Peach, tries to think of new tactics to keep Peach hers alone. She takes another drink of Diet Coke and then pulls a cigarette case engraved with the image of a lake out of her handbag.

"I know who I am," Peach says, but her statement isn't exemplified by her quiet tone.

Patti freezes, setting down the little silver box. "Excuse me? Wise to the entire world, are we Peach? No one has a real identity at nineteen. I'm fifty-one years old and I still wonder who I am. Don't be stupid, Peach. You have no clue. This is just you getting in your jabs, trying to show me up. I understand your game and I won't play it. Won't play it at all!"

Peach buries her face in the flowers, the satiny petals of the roses cup her chin and she swallows to keep from coughing again at the scent of the yarrow. She whispers into the blooms a wish for something better.

She whispers, "I am Peach Barrow. I will own my life. I am special, powerful, and full of energy. This life of mine *is* mine."

But she can't help herself from hedging her bets, just like she plans to do with Adam and how she has for years with Patti.

"Someday."

SPRING, 2014

63   RILEY

Not only does he try to use the same condom twice, he tries
to use it with two different girls. It's not exactly a threesome
Riley engages in; the women are separated by a piece of free-
standing bamboo screen that folds in at sharp angles, cutouts in
the wood covered in rice paper. The ladies are roommates,
college girls at Boise State, and Riley doesn't remember which
one he came home with because he'd been deep in the bottle
when he made his play. Once he was in the small apartment with
the Jimi Hendrix poster on the inside front door and not only a
blue-glassed bong on the dresser, but a makeshift apple pipe in
the kitchen, he went for both of them. The girls had been
fighting, however, and were adamant they not engage one
another physically. Hence the barrier.

He does his best to juggle fucking the two women, zipping
around the room partition to lick a nipple before jumping up to
get his balls squeezed. The girls find the entire fiasco
entertaining, and when he leaves one woman for the next, each

breaks out into a fit of giggles fueled by pot and youth. Having spent himself in the brunette, he tries to keep the condom on for another go in the raven-haired roomie with the tiny breasts.

She catches him as he tries to force in the semen-filled tip and slaps him hard on the upper arm. He shrugs and rips off the condom before sticking his naked dick in her and choking her out until she comes.

"You on the pill?" he asks.

She leans back, languorously touching her chest. Her friend walks past the screen and scowls before picking her underwear out of her butt crack and taking long swigs of orange juice from a jug left out on the coffee table.

"I think so?" she says and stares at a string of green Christmas lights tacked to the popcorn-textured ceiling.

"Well if not," Riley laughs, "I have the money to take care of it." He slaps her hard on the belly and she winces and smiles.

He really does. Riley coming into a lot of cash was the sole benefit to his pillars of the community, well-to-do parents dying suddenly.

He stands up, cracks his back and walks naked to the one window overlooking a grassy area on the BSU campus.

"What are we wanting to eat tonight, ladies? Mushrooms or cocaine?"

The brunette wipes her mouth clean of the citrus juice and stares vacantly at Riley.

"I could do some coke. We could hit a club and all screw in a bathroom stall. I sort of even like Casey again."

The raven-haired woman keeps her eyes on the lights. "I'm down for it. Blow and sex. But this time in the ass."

Riley watches a group of boys toss a small yellow Frisbee around the common area outside. They have Nalgene water bottles hanging from carabineers on their belt loops. They take long drinks of what is likely vodka instead of water.

He turns and scratches himself. He's in love with zero

responsibility, smitten with his days without work, lustful about his windfall of cash. He feels free from the expectations of society, released when his parents were killed. He's burning like wildfire.

"Put on nice dresses. No rayon or spandex, ladies. Let's get some lobster first and then get fucked up."

FRIDAY, THE 17TH OF APRIL, 2015

PEACH

"You might actually need to see a counselor. Like one who doesn't consider you a friend. Someone you can talk to about the changes you're going through. Because I don't think I'm doing enough."

Camille, sits back in her ergonomic office chair, a box of takeout sweet and sour pork in her lap. She lifts a piece of meat to her lips with chopsticks and licks it clean of sauce before plunking it in her mouth.

Peach is jittery, bites at her cuticles on her fingers. She's running out of time to commit to her plan. And she needs a pep talk from Camille. They're becoming regular things, these mini-sessions when Peach has a lull between her own clients. But Camille keeps pressing for more specific information from Peach, and Peach is stubborn in her refusal to give it. They're at a stalemate and Peach considers yielding a little to Camille's questions, if only so she can get some insight into what might be keeping her from embracing her path to her new self completely and resolutely.

"No, Camille, really, you help so much," Peach says and hands her coworker a napkin from the plastic bag the meal was delivered in.

"Then let me really help you. Tell me what it is you're afraid of when it comes to changing your life? Change in general? A specific fear? Something has you frozen. I can tell by your body language, how you've been coming into work either exhausted or slightly maniac. You're wrestling with a decision. Standing at a crossroads, right?"

Camille ignores her meal for a moment. "Look in my eyes, Peach. Dead on into them. Right now."

Peach tilts her head back and exhales sharply, but then she does what Camille asks of her. She's shocked at the tears that prick up and slip out of her lids when she engages the woman fully. Camille doesn't respond to the crying and maintains her hard stare.

"What are you afraid of?"

Peach thinks of Nell, the way her body moves to the tune of money and men, how she's a prize to be won, all other competitors to be outsmarted or outplayed even if they don't know they're in the game. And then the idea of Nell fades and it's replaced by a vision of Peach. But it's not the Peach who's present, sitting across from Camille and her Chinese food. It's a Peach of elemental strength, ritualized power and universal knowledge.

It's Perfect Peach.

It comes out then, without thought.

"I'm afraid of myself," Peach says. "Of me. I'm terrified of me."

Camille breaks her eye contact then and tosses the white takeout box in the trash. She flips on a candle warmer next to her seat and shakes her head at Peach.

"What?" Peach says. "I'm serious."

"You're shallow," Camille responds, "but it's better than what you've given me before. You can start with it."

"How?" Peach asks, able to give advice to her own clients, but blinded by her own problems, just like everyone else.

"I say you use the Peach you want to become as the motivator. This new ideal of yourself can become your taskmaster of sorts. If you don't stick to your goals and dreams, new Peach will be disappointed in you. She'll chide you for your laziness or lack of commitment. Ruler to the knuckles type of thing."

Peach smiles a bit at the idea. It's clever, really. To use the Peach she aspires to become as the catalyst for her transformation. Ends, or end in this case, causing all of the means. Perfect Peach wouldn't accept failure or backing down. Perfect Peach *is* someone to fear when that fear produces action. And those actions will bring her into being.

"I think you'd be reported for giving that advice to one of your clients," Peach takes her fingertips away from her face, tears flicked to the carpet, and tucks her hands under her seat. "But it's genius. I get it."

Her coworker reaches over and punches Peach lightly on the thigh. "Girlie, if you're not happy being you and want to change your path in life, let that future Peach keep you on the right track. Future existence, prompting current existence, so the future state can occur. It's enough for a metaphysical treatise. I think I should have been a philosopher. Or a screenwriter. I could sell a script to Christopher Nolan."

Peach hops up and gives her coworker a hug. She can tell Camille is stunned by the physical affection and pats Peach lightly on the back.

"I'm feeling horrible," Peach says matter-of-factly. "I'm rescheduling my appointment with Michel and going home. I think my chow mein was off. I'm dire sick."

Camille flicks her hand at Peach and winks. "Right. Sick.

Got it."

Peach leaves Camille, tidies up her office, gathers up the folders she needs to take home. They are cases requiring attention later, when her body isn't shaking with potential. Thoughts batter her mind but she staves them off, letting in only those beliefs concerning capability and invincibility, impetus and journeys.

She exits the glass doors of the office building and can hear the serenade of the frog, his slimy body hidden somewhere nearby. Perhaps her client, Michel, is with the amphibian. Perhaps he watches her aglow with the splendor that comes with knowing her path. Her face is one massive grin, her chest pitched to the clouds above.

This is Peach, ecstatic in her overwhelming, outrageous fear of letting herself down.

SATURDAY, THE 18TH OF APRIL, 2015

65   RILEY

A hail storm slants its icy bullets straight into the tall, double-paned windows of Riley's bedroom. He moves to his dresser, a heavy piece of oak with leafy tendrils cut into the front panels. It was his father's chest of drawers, one of the things he kept before he had the estate sale to liquidate his parents' belongings. He pulls open the top drawer where he keeps his boxer-briefs. The wallpaper-esque drawer liner is from the seventies; chartreuse and yellow daisies cover it. The inside smells of musky cologne and dry wood. It smells like his father, Will Wanner.

Riley lifts up a pile of his underwear and tucks the three cards from Hamal under the fabric. He intends to forget about the messages. He vows to stop rereading the contents of the cards. He swears to stop caring.

With that behind him, Riley gets ready for bed, flossing his teeth with cinnamon-flavored floss. He trims his nose hairs and takes an electric shaver to his upper cheeks and cleans away his partial sideburns. A shower with a plastic bag tied around his left foot, then a bit of Acqua di Gio on his neck so it's faded a bit by morning and he's ready for sleep.

He props his left foot up on the bed, each day closer to ditching his crutches. The small line of ink the tattooist managed to get in him is capped by a thread of black scabbing. He lies with his right foot and right arm hanging over the bed. He puts his left hand on his stomach and can feel the muscle there, taut, though he's been remiss in his exercising since the accident.

Time shifts, the room stays solidly black because of an absent moon. And Riley knows, when he wakes in the morning, he will restart a life of fun and freedom. Tomorrow he will start again. He'll have sex with Nell, somehow, and the man Riley wants to be again will rise, like the fantastical phoenix, feral and still smoking from the fire.

66   PEACH

She wishes she could spend more time with the growing lamb. She comes home each day to find a mess of hay scattered around the tarpaulin she tacked down over the living room rug. Still, the area is festooned with bits of fuzz, slobber and the occasional bathroom mishap. Worse yet is the way the baby looks at her, hopeful with tail high when she enters the room and prone to bleating whenever she leaves. She can only imagine the anxiety and fear the lonely creature feels away from his flock, with his shepherd busy with other pressing matters.

But there's nothing to be done about it now. She intends to keep the ram, at least for a while. Peach hopes the baby doesn't cry the entire time she's gone, resulting in someone deciding to complain to the apartment management. She won't let the lamb be taken from her. On this point she is immovable.

Peach sits inside the cordoned off area of her living room and the lamb folds his legs and sits happily in her open lap. The creature is already domesticated and attached to her. It worries her that something so fragile trusts her to watch it, feed it. The lamb still doesn't have a name. She can't decide what it should be, what would be an appropriate name for the creature she snatched away from its mother on Easter morning. Jesus would be too snide. Wooly and Harry too cutesy and on the nose. So she forgoes any title and dips her head down to nuzzle her chin in his soft coat.

"I've got a day left," she says to the animal. "Just a day to make the ultimate change and take what's rightfully mine. If it doesn't happen for me tomorrow with Nell, I have one other option. And if that doesn't work, I'm finished. There will never be a Perfect Peach. You'll be sent to a petting zoo and I'll be resigned to my life."

The lamb takes up one of her fingers in his mouth and sucks gently on it. His jaw grinds at her bone but there is no pain.

"Let's make the stars proud of us tomorrow," she says. "Let me be afraid enough of letting down Perfect Peach, my future self, that I have no other way to go but forward."

The animal's bleating is the only response. She hugs the lamb tight to her body and she can hear a steady pounding of hail, imagines how it flattens the browned, spent daffodils outside her home.

67   RILEY

Riley dreams of sex with Nell. The dream is silent and full of muted colors. She lies in the middle of a river bed lined with smooth, round rocks, water flowing around her pale body. There isn't any clothing on her frame and her fake breasts ride high on her chest, her sex shorn clean of hair.

He kneels down in the water. It's frigid, nearly ice, and bits of leaves and tree bark sail past him on the water's surface. Nell's face is turned away from his. She looks over her shoulder, her gaze on something upon the river bank. Riley looks and can see a row of trout, some brown, some rainbow, spitted on a length of willow and then stuck in one of the gaps on a well-balanced, tall rock cairn. Their open mouths face the sky, their tails flaccid and delicate, dipping to earth.

With her attention focused on the fish, Riley pushes his way inside the woman and works at her gently, looking for the cadence of his pleasure. But the intimacy is uninspired and weak and he can claim no end to his task. He plunges, thrusts, and Nell keeps her eyes on the fish.

He can't feel his legs or his pelvis and he thinks it's because of the cold water. Soon, his penis is also dead, but he still resolutely keeps at the act. He looks down in the water and his lower body is starkly white, blue veins bulging along the surface of his skin.

And then he can suddenly feel sensations again in his groin and he pulls Nell's hips closer to him, only to find her hips have changed in size. They are thinner, with a bony pelvic bone he handles with clumsy fingers. Looking up her frame, the breasts have changed. Now they are a bit smaller and softly natural and the red asymmetrical locks are gone, replaced by a short mop of blond hair.

It's not Nell at all anymore. It's someone else that he cannot name but knows intimately already. His penis pricks back to life and when he reaches climax, the woman turns to look into his blue eyes and smiles.

"Go fish," she says.

He collapses on her chest and kicks his legs out in the water, until the current forces his legs upstream and he can see both his feet. The left foot tingles, pulsates, and then before his eyes, his toes sprout anew, bone worming out of the puckered scars. Muscle oozes out of the small holes that pockmark the surface of the bone. And then flesh crackles to life over the striated meat. Nails push free of the skin and Riley is left with a healed foot, a miracle.

The woman sits up and extends her arms to him. He gladly falls backwards into her body and then she lays them both back into the cold of the river, half their faces submerged, their bodies spooning, their limbs tangled in a mess of life.

68 PEACH

Peach dreams of Nell wearing a dress of golden fleece, a pair of twisting horns growing from her temples. In Peach's arms are a spread of apples, tufts of grass held together with tied dandelion stems, chunky blocks of salt. She lays her offerings in front of Nell, who gyrates her body on a stage set up in a field of alfalfa. The plants are capped with vivid purple blossoms. But the woman wants nothing of what she has brought and continues to dance, ambivalent to the gifts. Peach falls to the field, to her knees.

A fire spontaneously ignites far away from the stage, yards and yards away in the field of alfalfa. Peach watches the red and yellow flicker gain force and height. It consumes the plants in its area and then moves in the direction of the stage. She knows it is not a normal fire, that it contains intelligence, because when it sets its current fuel to ash, it cuts a straight line to Nell and Peach.

Apprehension and woe churn within Peach and she knows

she's running out of time. The fire will reach both the women soon and when it does, it will consume them. Peach lifts herself from the dirt and climbs up on the stage to face the dancer.

"Why do you call yourself Nell Hyde?" she asks her.

The dancer responds with a kick of her heels together, a shaking of her torso down to the hard platform. Peach can see the fire approaching, surging for them.

"I need you," Peach says to the woman.

Nell's face remains unexpressive, but then she turns her back to Peach. There, right under the short hair of her A-line cut, is a mouth nestled in the fold where skull meets neck. It opens, showing red gums, red tongue, teeth stained red with blood.

"You don't want me for me," the head speaks and then smiles.

The fire is close, closing on them, already scorching half of the field which stretches to the hazy horizon. Its hunger is insatiable, its speed remarkable.

Peach pleads with the macabre maw set in the head. "You're the first key and with you, I'll take back what's mine."

"There are many doors with many keyholes and many keys." the mouth answers. "So set on me. Foolish Peach!"

When the fire reaches them, the ground is no longer rows of green and brown and purple, but alive with heat and licks of flame. A spark jumps high enough to ignite the golden wool around Nell's body. She is alight with fire, her skin melting from her skeleton. The lips open once more for Peach.

"Take it from him," it says before Nell's flaming corpse explodes into a supernova of energy and Peach, her body gone as well, floats in the void of space, a milky screen of stars behind her consciousness and the energy of human life, a bomb of light and potential, throbbing before her.

SUNDAY, THE 19TH OF APRIL, 2015

69   RILEY

The dream is so vivid that when he wakes, Riley pulls the sheets off his body and bolts up to look at his left foot. He slips the gauze off, looping it around his fingers before just giving up and letting it twirl into a pool on his bed sheet. But he finds only his wounded foot, the sticky points of the stitching, the toes absent.

Even though his toes didn't regenerate, he smiles to the empty room and lies back in bed. He knows today will be the first day of his new life and he doesn't feel bad thinking it cliché. No more work. He can coast on the dregs of his bank account and unemployment coupled with the disability checks he might receive because of his lost toes, at least for a time. Because tomorrow he might be caught in a fiery truck or in a herd of panicking animals. These potential vehicles for pain and death play on repeat in his mind now. He cannot shake them but he doesn't mean for them to take hold in reality, either.

The dream is already slipping his mind, but he does

remember he was having sex with Nell and he vows again to make another move tonight. Sev can be distracted and Nell wooed. He looks at his foot again, at the unfinished tattoo. That, too, will be remedied this evening.

Riley feels like he has a handle on life this midmorning Sunday. He shoots his arms straight into the air, clenches his fists at nothing but holds on tightly, until his nails put little crescent moons into his flesh.

70   PEACH

The bouncer takes her money and tells her she looks extra nice this evening. Peach looks down the length of her red dress, the same one she wore to dinner with Linx weeks ago. The yielding fabric hugs the sides of her breasts and runs over the slight curve of her hips and ass. She smiles at the man and walks into the din and dim lights of Blaze Lounge, a black clutch bag tucked under her arm. Her eyes meter the actions of the room and find Sev and Nell drinking at the bar.

Peach smoothes out her dress, careful not to step on the hem with her heels. She feels trepidation at moving toward the couple. She knows she must, but all her careful planning, all her machinations as to how to get Nell away from Sev suddenly seem childish and uncouth.

There is only one thing she knows she must do. All other means and options are mutable; Peach realizes she might need to get creative and work with the way events unfold.

It's Nell who sees Peach and waves at her, motions for her

255

to come to the bar and join the duo. Peach grins, pinching up and in at the fabric at her waist so she might walk more smoothly. The attire is sleeveless so her arms are freezing but the material is synthetic, so the core of her body is deprived of airflow, sweat beading up and sandwiching itself between her skin and the gown.

When she reaches the two, they pull a stool around from the bar and place it between their seats. Sev winks at Peach and Nell slides off her perch and rummages around in a large canvas bag at her feet. She flings her arm into the air and a length of fabric follows. It's Peach's fleece jacket.

"Here," she says and pushes it into Peach's hands. The dancer's eyes are glassy, her face relaxed. Peach wonders how long the couple has been at the booze.

She can smell that the jacket hasn't been washed, still impregnated with the stink of old tobacco. "Thanks for bringing it to me," she says and shimmies onto the stool, tosses the jacket to the brass foot rest below and places her clutch in her lap.

"What are you drinking? Nell's shift is over for the night and you're going to go home with us." Sev waves over a petite bartender and waits for Peach's drink order.

"I'll have what you're drinking," she says and looks at the brown liquid in tall glasses in front of each of them. She has no intention to drink at all and will have to find a way to fake sipping at the alcohol. As to the comment about going home with the pair, she decides to stay mute for now.

"Dirty Aussie," Nell says and touches a length of some of Peach's hair.

"Is that the name of the drink?" Peach asks, her skin tingling from Nell's caresses.

"No," Sev laughs, "she's talking about me. She loves me even though I'm a bludger." Then the dancer and the poet give into their mirth, laugh heartily for a few minutes and Peach knows they're probably too drunk to notice she won't be drinking.

The bartender sets the drink on a bar napkin in front of Peach and Sev swiftly lifts the glass off the napkin and snatches it away, adding it to a pile of them to be inked with his poems. He turns his legs in toward Peach and she can feel Nell do the same thing. Their attention makes her squirm a bit, think about her options on running away. Their energy presses at her and she feels like the filling of a sandwich, ready to go spilling out the sides.

Nell's outfit is comprised of a tube top in bright green and sequined boy shorts in black. Her shoes have been kicked off onto the floor and she lets her painted toes dangle from the stool. She's curled her hair into tight ringlets and a tube of bangles runs up her left arm.

"I like your dress," she tells Peach and leans in to rub at the fabric. "The color really suits you."

Sev cuts off Peach's reply. "It suits the carpet in our bedroom even better."

And this gets the partners to lock eyes, their game of lust and a potential threesome more exciting to play with one another than the actual act might be. Peach clicks the plastic knobs open on her clutch and palms a bottle in her hand. She closes her fist around the orange plastic and decides to change the subject.

"So who's the best dancer here, Nell?" Peach says and swivels around on her stool to look at the stage. Two women dance on the raised dais. One has skin the color of tawny sand. The other has three piercings in her belly button.

When Sev and Nell turn to look at the stage, Peach does her best to unscrew the cap on the bottle while the pair vocalize unkind criticisms of the strippers doing their best. Her hands shake and her fingers do sloppy work. She gets the top off one side only and she fumbles the container. She catches it in time, preventing the contents from spilling on the floor.

She turns her body slightly back to the stage and agrees

blindly to what they've said and then points out the kinds of shoes the girls are wearing, which sets Sev off on a diatribe about women's fashion, aristocracy and deception.

"It's cold in here," Peach says and reaches down for the returned jacket. With her body dipped under the bar, she opens the bottle completely and pours out the contents into her palm. She pulls the fleece up to her lap and rests her closed fist in its folds, white powder held in her grasp.

Her throat is so tight she must force a swallow. She looks around the room and while Sev and Nell are still distracted, she drops half of the white powder into Nell's drink and the other half into Sev's. She has no idea how much of the crushed Ambien she's given them. But as the tasteless, ground-up sleeping pills sink down into the dark liquid of their glasses, Peach knows there is no going back.

She dusts her hands together to send the remains of the powder to the floor and reminds herself not to rub her fingers on her mouth or into her eyes. After tonight, she'll never want to go back.

Peach touches Nell on the shoulder, then brushes Sev's thigh, and points to their drinks. "So I'm actually new to drinking. I've had wine once but hard liquor? I don't know if I will be able to stomach it. I've seen people pound drinks, of course. Do you mind showing me how to get it down in one go so I don't gag on the taste?"

The poet picks up his booze and puts a hand on Peach's thigh. "New to strip clubs. New to alcohol. The enchantress has led a monastic life all these years." Then he and Nell slip the liquid down their throats, mouths open wide like fledglings await a meal, and drop their spent glasses back to the bar.

"I guess it's never too late for you to catch up and be naughty. Before the night's done you'll be showing us your fanny," Sev says as he wipes his mouth with the edge of a napkin already penned with a poem. Peach can see the words "serpentine" and "quixotic" as he blots his lips before returning the napkin to a soft stack of written treasures.

Laying her hand over his, Peach turns to look at Nell's lips and then, her eyes. She only holds contact briefly before switching her gaze to the drink in front of her. The brown liquid dallies around chucks of sharp ice and the pink and blue lights of the stage hit the glass. Other shots of colored light zip across the plane of the dark wood bar.

"I thought it time to start," Peach says.

71   RILEY

He doesn't ask Walker to join him at Blaze Lounge tonight. He senses his friend is tired of Riley's overdependence on him since the accident. And besides, Riley has his tattoo appointment later in the evening and has decided to do it alone. Unless, of course, Nell is along for the ride. And Riley has every intention of making that potential a fantastic reality.

He gets past the doorman without an issue, showing him his ID while keeping his face pointed down so the bouncer can't smell the whisky on his breath. He can't afford to lose entry to the club because he's perceived as being too hammered. And while he shouldn't have driven after polishing off a half of a fifth at home, fun, free and wild Riley doesn't worry about things like DUIs and criminal records. He didn't worry before. He wouldn't now.

Once his eyes adjust to the lack of light in the club, Riley immediately sees Nell at the bar with her boyfriend and another woman whom he doesn't recognize. He smirks, emboldened by the booze and a level of horniness he hasn't felt since getting his toes smashed, and he moves to the little group.

The woman he doesn't know catches a glimpse of him coming and turns her back to him. Sev, the belligerent poet, stands to head Riley off, but stumbles a bit and catches himself on his bar stool. It's Nell's response that shocks Riley. Having always given him the cold shoulder and looks of unveiled disgust, tonight she stands too upon his arrival, nearly as wobbly as her partner, and reaches out to Riley.

He steps into her embrace and she twines her arms around him and takes a deep sniff of his neck. "You smell good," she says. She sways a bit and Riley has to move his injured foot out of the way of her bare feet.

"Thanks, sweetie," he says and then gently pries her hands away from him. Sev is glaring at him when he can get his eyes to focus for longer than a second on a single point of interest. Riley cocks his head at their drunken behavior. They're so inebriated he wonders if they've taken a narcotic or opiate along with their alcohol.

Sev speaks, his words slurred and slow. "What is it you're wearing, mate? There was a koala bear in my grandmother's backyard in Queensland. It would scream at other koalas. Scream!"

Riley is tipsy but even he knows what the poet is saying is off base and irrelevant. Nell sways in front of Riley, so close to him the tips of her breasts rub at his shirt. He resists the urge to reach up and fondle the stripper in front of her boyfriend. But with the way the poet is acting, he's not sure the man would even notice, and if he did notice, even care in his altered state.

The woman with the long blond hair keeps her face away from Riley but reaches out a hand to steady Nell, holding her lightly at the hip bone. Sev puts both hands on the stool and puffs out his chest.

"Do you know those koalas are filthy little beasts? They

pass chlamydia to one another. Their genitals are covered in STDs and they fuck one another while high on eucalyptus leaves."

Nell hiccoughs. "I need to pee."

And that's when Sev covers the distance between he and Riley, knocking the blond's shoulder hard as he passes and pushing Nell back into the woman's lap. Riley smells cigarette smoke in the man's hair and watches as a vein in his neck expands and beats in time with his heart. Though Riley expects the poet's heart to pump wildly with anger, the muscle in his chest must be working lethargically. The man has several inches, a hundred pounds on Riley.

"You're trying to pass your filthy dick to my girl," Sev sprays a bit of spit onto Riley's face.

Riley tightens his hands, ready for a brawl. He won't back down now. He'll have Nell tonight and his life will be the better for it.

"Yes," he responds, "and she'll take it tonight."

Instead of the punch Riley expects, or a yell of rage, Sev spurts out a laugh, then holds his lips closed with his fingers to try and contain himself. His legs fold under him and he sits crossed-legged on the floor, hand grasping the ankle of Riley's left leg as he chuckles.

Riley picks up his leg and tries to shake him off but the man's grip is steely. He hopes the poet won't think to smash a fist into his wounded foot. After a moment, he decides to stay still and let the man hold him. He doesn't feel trapped. He can detach, escape at any time.

72   PEACH

The dancer is rocking around on her sequin-covered ass, pressing into Peach's lap and Peach whispers into her ear, cautious to not let the man named Riley see too much of her face. She hadn't planned on him being at the club, but it's the first chink in her plot for this evening. She knew there were many potential challenges ahead of her and after slipping Sev and Nell the Ambien, her actions would be at the whim of the effects of the sleep aid and the alcohol. She didn't foresee having to deal with competition tonight for Nell's attention. She reminds herself to be flexible, to take whatever path leads her to her one immovable goal.

"Let's get you to the bathroom. Put some cool water on your face," she says and then stands up, lifting her weight and the dancer's as well. Peach's arms wrap around the woman to prevent her from slumping to the floor. The woman's legs are flaccid and Peach has to encourage her to stiffen her joints by running the back of her hands along the back of Nell's knees.

Riley is locked to the floor by a giggling Sev and tries his best not to look concerned about the odd scene. His eyes meander about the bar and he plays it cool. But she can see from the slight wobble in his torso, he's far from sober as well. Peach uses the time to turn Nell's body toward the back of the club and the hallway to the bathroom.

As she maneuvers the woman through the tables, men sling comments at them and one reaches out a few fingers to pinch Nell's behind. He misses though, and catches her upper thigh. But the woman doesn't have the presence of mind to stop and protest or slap at the man. The pair moves forward, guided by the pressure and direction of Peach.

When they get to the bathroom, Peach is happy to find it vacant and she pushes open the door and then escorts Nell inside. Once in, she depresses the little circular locking mechanism to shut them inside and then lets Nell go, free to stumble around the one room with its open toilet and free-standing sink. The stripper goes to the toilet and pulls down her boy shorts before squatting on the bowl. Peach turns away and pretends to check her lip gloss in the mirror.

"That Riley is quite the asshole, right?" she asks the dancer. When she doesn't get a response she ventures a look at Nell on the toilet and finds her asleep, shorts around her lower thighs with her chin cupped in her hands.

Peach freezes, not sure if she should wake her or if now is the time, if she should do what she needs to do to Nell, here in Blaze Lounge. It is the best place to carry out her task, but leaves much to be desired in terms of privacy. She turns her head skyward and tries to bring a map of the stars to her inner vision, imagine them shimmering in the cosmos outside the club.

"Now?" she asks the universe out loud, her eyes shut, her heart thumping. "Shall I do it now?

"He's not an asshole," Nell answers and Peach's eyes fly open to see the woman lifting herself off the toilet and shuffling to the sink. She doesn't flush her urine and her shorts remain around her legs until she turns on the tap and looks down to see them binding her movements.

Peach was expecting this, had heard of cases where people on Ambien actually sleepwalk, have conversations and do high-functioning activities like driving. But they're mentally asleep, unable to remember what they've done. And when she found out this bit of information, she was hopeful the dancer would experience this loss of memory. She needs Sev to experience it, too. Her plans depend on the strength of a forced, chemical slumber.

Nell reaches down to tug up her shorts and falls doing so, pitching forward and to her left. Peach can see her wobble but does nothing to stop the accident. The stripper's head passes dangerously close to the side of the sink. An inch or so closer and she would have cracked her skull as she fell. But she's fine, just slightly confused in a jumble on the floor.

That's when Peach takes a breath and moves to help her up, thoughts of the woman's head opening up like in her dream, at the back of her skull, a mouth of red poised to argue about Peach's actions. She reaches her arms down to the woman and she climbs Peach's frame to get back on her feet. As she does, Peach's hand comes into contact with the woman's bare ass and she lets it stay there for a moment.

"You like it, don't you?" Nell says to Peach and then moves into Peach, her eyes sleepy, her mouth pursing into a bow.

Then a knock sounds at the bathroom door, then three sharp raps, and Sev's voice is yelling through the locked wooden door.

"Get out here, Nell," he screams. "Come choose who you want to fuck."

73 RILEY

After watching the women take off for the bathroom, Riley
felt Sev abruptly unlatch himself and noted his staggered-stepped
march to the bathroom hallway in pursuit. Unwilling to let the
prospect of winning Nell go, he followed the poet to the door of
the women's toilet.

Sev pounds away at the wood, calling for Nell to emerge
while spewing random quotes from Keats and Byron.

"These two are from Keats," he hollers, puts all his girth
against the door. *"My love is selfish. I cannot breathe without
you.* And this one. *I was never afraid of failure; for I would
sooner fail than not be among the greatest!"*

Riley looks to the bar and to the bouncer speaking to a
cluster of underage boys, but no one moves to halt the
commotion. The poet keeps knocking, his fist turning purple
from the impact and his face twisting into layers of wrinkled
flesh.

The door swings open and Sev rears back to keep from

266

falling forward, his bulk held aloft by the door. Nell comes out first and flails out with her arms, pushing Sev away from her trajectory and stumbling toward where Riley stands a few feet away.

The other woman starts out the door but Sev, his weight unmanageable with whatever drink and drugs he's had, crashes into the woman as she enters the hallway. They go down together, Sev's mass covering her delicate frame.

And then Nell is on Riley, her face pressed against his throat, her torso squirming as he leans into her. She mutters something he can't make out due to the panels of long hair near her face, obscuring the sound of her inebriated mumbling.

"Come again?" he says and moves the hair away so he can look down at her face. Her lips droop slightly and her mascara is smeared across her eyelids.

"Let's go," she says again. "I want to get out of here and get on all fours."

And then she reaches between Riley's legs and rubs the meat of her palm against his privates.

He grins.

74 PEACH

The poet's weight is crushing her. She wriggles to get out from under him but his bulk and height pin her down. His limbs are slack and uncontrolled. He moves like a snake, exactly what she considers him, inching his torso forward just enough to line his face up with Peach's. Sev gives her a wink, his lid slow to move over his eyeball. He smells like the piquant scent of juniper berries turned to gin coupled with cigarette smoke. The combination of odors makes her think of the night she lit the fireworks downtown. She is close. Too close to let the weight of someone so clueless immobilize her.

"I just want to protect her from that douche," he gets out, a line of drool escaping his mouth and landing on Peach's nose. She brings her hands up to try and wipe it away but can't get past his head.

"I get it," she sighs, "but he's not the one she needs protection from."

Sev's eyes widen and after a moment, she can feel the man

growing hard, his penis pressing into the softness of her upper thigh. His face contracts and Peach wonders if he's experiencing a moment of lucidity from the sleeping pills.

"I know you want her. You go down on her and I'll write poetry while I mount you from behind."

Peach curls her lips back and turns her head to escape the man's eyes. "You're no poet. You're a snake. And though I don't know much about literature, I do know a lot about mythology. And in the end, you lose."

"Lose what?" he says and Peach can feel his body going slack on her, the vigor in his pants subsiding. She uses the last of her resolve to press up hard and shift under him. After a couple tries she finds the right angle of escape and rolls free of his body. She gains her feet and looks down at the man. He doesn't move at all and she hopes he's finally passed out.

She walks stiffly, quickly back to the bar, not wanting to run and make others suspicious or nervous. She picks up her fleece jacket and her purse and then looks around for Nell and Riley. She sees them, at the door, passing the bouncer who thinks nothing of the limp stripper draped around the shoulders of a man who's not her boyfriend.

"No," Peach says to the room and she must decide whether or not to make a scene, to get the woman away from the man. But in the end she knows she can't chance getting in the man's face and taking away his prize. If she does, he'll remember her for sure. Remember how he hit on her weeks ago. And then she'll be etched in his mind.

That can't happen. Not yet.

She watches them open the door to the night air, the headlights of a car in the parking lot blinking on and off, its alarm sounding into the dark.

75   RILEY

He props her up against the side of his Nissan so he can
open up the passenger door and help her inside. He's having
problems seeing straight, the world a blurry, haloed mess, but
even so he knows the dancer is completely blitzed. This doesn't
deter his objectives though; he's determined to have her, no
matter the circumstances.

She does a little dance against the metal of the car, her eyes
shut, her tube top riding up her back from the friction of rubbing
against the vehicle.

"You know I had a dream about you last night," Riley slurs,
"and I took you in it. We were in a river having sex. And I knew
it had to come true, the sex part. That getting you, coming here,
this all leads to my new life and the new me. It's beginning,
sweetie."

Nell continues to slither against the car and she works off
her shoes without bending down. Her pelvis tilts forward and she
runs her hands over her bare stomach. He nearly lands on his ass

when he stoops down to pick up her footwear. Riley crawls back
up her legs, pausing to lick a kneecap, strappy heels hanging off
his thumb. He regains his equilibrium and waits for her to say
something.

When she opens her eyes they don't focus on him or
anything close by. They stare off into the middle distance, her
lips slightly parted.

"It was my birthday a few days ago," she says, still dancing.
"I'm so old. Twenty-five! People centuries ago were grandmas
by my age. Or at least pretty close to being grandmas. They
weren't swinging around metal poles. No way. But I'm the
birthday girl. That's what Sev has been saying all week, calling
me 'Birthday Girl Nell.' I'm an Aries."

He cocks his head and puts his hands on her squirming hips.
"That's your zodiac sign?"

She nods yes and keeps rambling. "I'm a perfect Aries. I'm
fiery and bold and someday I could totally be a leader. My sign
is the ram. A sheep. It doesn't make sense, though. Sheep are
animals meant to be killed or shaved or herded. They don't rule
the world. I wonder how many grandmothers have ruled the
world?"

She nuzzles up to his body and Riley's face, usually red
from drink, turns a deeper scarlet from excitement and the
promise of sex. Some ill-remembered Bible quote comes to mind
about the meek and being like lambs and inheriting the planet.
He can't recall the gist of it well enough and doesn't care to
stumble through a lame rendition of it with Nell. He has
something more appropriate to say in response.

"Maybe the important thing is the ramming," he says and
snickers at his own joke. He runs a hand up her inner thigh and
then points her to the open door of the car.

"When I was a tiny baby, I had no one," she says apropos of
nothing. Her head rolls around on her neck before she turns on
her bare soles and climbs into the SUV. Her body falls onto the

backseat and she goes fetal, tucking her heels against her ass.

Riley slams the door when all her limbs are inside. Winning is at hand. The woman mutters something else through the glass. Something about the numbers on his license plate but he doesn't ask her what she's on about. He's headed to his own door, his own seat, his own success.

76   PEACH

The white Nissan nearly backs over Peach. She notices
when the car turns and lurches forward that Nell is slumped in
the back seat, her head barely visible, and Riley sits upright at
the wheel. He's close to it, like the steering wheel is his intended
lover, and he clutches it with both hands. She watches them go,
fighting back the urge to cry out.

A cluster of robins chirp as they dip low in their flight over
her head. They land in a ratty poplar near the parking lot. Except
for a solitary robin which takes post on the sign for Blaze
Lounge abutting Main Street. It holds one of its legs high, bent at
the joint, and trills out a series of calls in Peach's direction. It is
too dark outside for her to see the mass of cherry-colored
feathers on the bird's belly.

She looks up, to her friends overhead, and finds fortification
in the glow of the stars. The lights of downtown obscure them,
but she knows they're up there and they're rooting for her.

"I won't give up. Not after coming so far," she says to them and then gets in her Honda and peels out of the lot after the escaping duo.

She follows behind them for a time, not wanting to get too close though she figures Riley is too drunk to know he's being tailed. She considers calling the cops and reporting him drunk driving, but then she realizes there are only a few hours left in the day and involving the police would be the worst proverbial fuel to throw on the fire. They would likely detain Nell for questioning and Peach would be no better off.

The Nissan stops at a red light in a four-way intersection. But instead of staying behind the pair, Peach makes a crucial, calculated decision. She flips into the right lane and heads up 9th Street, a curving boulevard which takes her toward the Boise Train Depot and the neighborhoods sprawled across the Bench.

She gets there just as he's pulling down shades over the west-facing front windows flanking the entrance. This time the sign is illuminated and she can clearly see the words *Crucible Tattoo* in white lettering. She turns off her ignition and stares at the word "crucible." She knows the word has many meanings, but she only thinks of it in one way now. She envisions a sturdy bowl used for melting down metals. A crucible is subjected to fire time and time again and remains solid and strong.

The tattooist comes out the front door and squints at her sitting in the car. When she pushes open her door, he shakes his head and walks back inside. She follows him until he holds his ground just inside the doorway, preventing her from entering the parlor.

"You're not my appointment. No way you're getting a tattoo."

The man wears low-riding jean shorts in the cool of mid spring and Peach can see a shock of colorful ink winding down the left side of his neck and down his shirt. It's a visage she had memorized, at the beseeching of the stars. She was glad she had looked into the man. It had made her decision to turn away from her pursuit of Riley and Nell a bit easier.

She puts her hands in the air and then presses her palms together.

"Please," she begs, "it's super simple. And if you had another appointment that didn't show, take me instead."

"Where's it go?" the man asks.

"What?"

"On your body."

"Oh," Peach replies, the feeling of panic manifesting as roiling bile in her stomach. "On my head."

She moves her hands to the bloodstone pendant around her neck and asks for its energy to help her now, more than ever. Confidence. Self-esteem. Power.

"I ain't cutting your hair and shaving your head, girl. Put me an hour in before I get to inking and there's a house party I gotta hit before sleep. Hell no."

Without thinking, Peach lets go of her pendant and reaches up to the long hair on her head. She pulls at it roughly and the wig comes away in her hands. She holds the strawberry-tinged blond hair at her thighs and its strands cling to the static of her long dress. The skin of her head tingles in the cold and she reaches up to touch the sharp, half-inch growth of flaxen hair reaching stiffly to the sky.

The tattooist checks out her bare head from where he stands in the doorway. Then he nods slightly and turns his body aside so she can enter.

Old Peach tells her not to do it. Not to go inside. But Perfect Peach, the future Peach, the one who current Peach fears, picks up her feet and moves her forward.

When she crosses the threshold of the door, the man closes the glass behind them and walks around a counter with a cash register. He pulls out a clipboard of papers.

"You'll have to sign this shit," he says. "And you better not be drunk."

She takes the board from him, time seeming to move slowly. "I'm not," she promises.

He must be able to hear the soberness in her voice because he starts in on a story about a client, one who never showed up for his appointment tonight, and how he was drunk when he came in the first time looking to get tattooed.

"The dude bled everywhere. And then he begs for another appointment, says I'm the only one can tat the design he wants and then blows me off."

Peach signs all the papers and hands them back to the tattooist. He flips through the pages and skews his nose up at her signature.

"Weird name," he says and then puts the clipboard down on the counter. "I thought only rock stars went by one name?"

She doesn't reply, instead takes in the shop. There are a few chairs spread over an open room. What looks like a massage table is unfolded in a corner and the walls are lined with framed examples of tattoos that can be delivered to uninspired clients.

"Which one is your setup?"

He nods at a giant barber chair near the front counter and Peach approaches it cautiously. She wonders if she's alone with the man in the quiet of the shop.

"I've got to shave a little bit of your head," he says and spends some time gathering his supplies and tools and a disposable razor in navy blue. He snaps on a pair of black gloves the same color as the ink ready to tint her flesh. "Where's this thing going on your skull?"

Peach takes a seat and places her hand on the back of her head, where her neck flares up to her skull.

"Here," she says, "but it doesn't have to be too big. Just postage stamp-sized is fine. I would have done it myself, but if I don't have to, I might as well not screw it up."

"So you ink?" the man asks as he swabs her skin with a shock of cool rubbing alcohol. The smell transports her back to her bloody knees, back to trauma.

"No," she answers.

The tattooist takes her shoulders and tilts her away from him in the chair so he can access her scalp while seated on his rolling stool. He uses the razor in short, tight strokes to clean the new growth of hair off of her scalp. "Okay, so what are we doing?"

"The zodiac sign for Aries. The ram. It's like a V with curls at the top."

"Yeah, I know it. You want any fill, color, fading?"

"No, just simple black. Smallish."

He clicks his tattoo needle to life and braces one hand on Peach's back. "This is going to hurt, with all those tendons and nerves on your head. But it's only a few lines, so it'll be over quick. You ever get tattooed before?"

"No, but I plan on getting more. So I'll get through the pain."

The needle touches down and Peach tries her best not to jump. She feels every nerve ending down the length of her spine protest. She clutches the padded arm of the chair and grits her teeth.

The artist talks to her as he puts the black ink under her epidermis. "Isn't Ares the Greek god of war or something?"

"Yes," Peach replies, "but it isn't that Aries. The zodiac Aries is a ram. Though Ares the god is related to Mars. And Mars is the planet associated with this zodiac month. So I suppose there are two different entities, Aries and Ares, who have meaning right now."

"So it's some sheep? That's fucking lame," he says and then clicks off his needle. He's done quickly with the tattoo and the waves of pricking fire that inundated Peach dissipate and change to a sore aching.

"It's a ram," she says and turns in the chair to watch the tattooist unplug his needle and rest it on the tray with the other supplies. She can feel her scalp shimmer with power. She wishes she were outside, under the stars.

"You know a bunch about it," he says, looking down at his clean up, "you must be an Aries."

"No," she says, her voice strong.

He snorts a bit and unbuttons his high collar. "Lady, I didn't know all that and I should. I'm an Aries. Had a birthday twenty-four hours ago."

"I know," is all Peach says before whipping back her head and bringing it forward to butt the man soundly between his eyes.

The collision isn't the damaging blow she was looking for. The stool is on rollers and the force moves him backwards, absorbing most of the impact. He reaches up to his face and squints.

"Fuck!" he says and tries to stand.

Peach gets to her feet first and snatches the tattooing needle up, sending the tray flying, flipping over as it falls to the floor. While the man tries to pry open his watering eyes, Peach fits the contraption tightly in her hand and then plants it deep inside the man's left ear canal.

His scream is a piercing jab to her ears as he falls to the floor. His head narrowly misses the metal footrest of the barber chair. Peach rushes to silence him. Though she's light in frame and middling in height, she holds onto the chair arms and uses the strong leverage to bring her foot down on the tattooist's face, stomping hard with her heel until he goes quiet.

She forces herself to look at him then, to take in what she's done. She's dislodged a few teeth and his nose is sunken into a divot she's placed in his face with her high-heeled shoe. She doesn't think of him as a man any longer, but as a shell devoid of energy. His energy flows to her body. That essence now resides within her.

She bends down over his slack form and snaps on an extra

pair of surgical gloves which went spiraling to the floor when the tray tipped over during the attack. Depressing her fingers on his neck, she's relieved to find his pulse completely gone. She lifts her fingers away and sees she'd been pushing down on the tattoo of a warrior, a man clothed in leather, a sword slung over his back.

Dipping her fingers into the warm blood trickling out of the man's ear, she takes the blood, the life force of the man and reaches around to the new tattoo on her scalp. She massages the blood into her open pores, lets it mingle with her own blood. She thinks back to something she's thought of often during her transformation. Something she thought of when she was considering sacrificial rams and gods and energy exchange. She feels this is only right, she repeats in her mind; when a blood offering is made, your own blood is spilt as well. For her, right now, she bonds to the idea of not only spilt blood, but of a mark. A trophy, a sacred tattoo, consecrated with the life force of a sacred sacrifice.

She shoots upwards from where she crouches. In her pelvis, her nucleus of power, she feels a deeper thrum than before. Flares of sensation pour into each of her limbs from that epicenter and she knows she has unbolted the energy hidden there, buried deep for thirty-one years. She has added to it the power that once coursed through the sacrifice at her feet.

Perfect Peach would be, will be, is so proud.

"To beginnings!" she shouts down at the face of the dead man.

"To beginnings!" she shouts up through the ceiling and roof of Crucible Tattoo.

Up and out to the universe.

ACKNOWLEDGMENTS

To the humans who have always looked to the stars and seen stories written there, I am proud to carry on your work and share your myths. To my family, friends and support team that cheered me on and worked with me to bring this book to life, I cannot thank you all enough. And lastly, but in no way least, I am indebted to my guides. A hearty round of applause to you all. I raise a glass to the heavens.

CYCLE 2 OF *THE BLOOD ZODIAC*

CONTINUES WITH

THE BULL

01   PEACH

She can't get the blood out of her blond wig.

The natural hair must have been tinted the hue of honey by the wig-makers, because the blood seems to cling to it, color it. She convinces herself that hair exposed to peroxide might be subject to discoloring. Whether or not she's correct in her assumption, the locks appear ruddier now. If this is simply her imagination and the hair is unchanged, she cannot see clearly. Perhaps she witnesses some mysterious afterimage of the red liquid instead, a specter of that glorious act.

The wig in her hands meant to hide away her shorn scalp, the new tattoo at the base of her skull, these are potent, physical reminders of what she did to the tattooist just an hour ago. She had killed him. And she doesn't think of her action as wanton murder.

It had been a premier sacrifice.

While most of his blood—Roman Saucedo's blood—

ended up on the vinyl floor of the tattoo parlor, some of it splashed onto the seat of the barber chair where she'd cast off her hairpiece, leaving it an insentient witness to the violent thrusts of Peach's heel on the face of the man who had inked her with the sign of Aries. She scours the strands with a nail brush in the shape of a hedgehog and generous dollops of liquid dish soap. Her hands are white and puckered from the water and friction. A pool of pink liquid sloshes over the side of the kitchen sink, escapes the tub of dyed hair and suds, and plunks in steady drops on her bare toes. Twenty minutes into her task, she wonders why she doesn't use shampoo.

The young ram bleats from the living room, his cries a plea for milk and attention.

"Wait, baby," she coos to him.

After a few more minutes of scrubbing at the blotches of light strawberry marring her wig, she gives up, leaves it to soak, and pulls out a chrome-legged chair at her little mid-century dining table. Her body feels heavy, the adrenaline nearly spent. It's only now she'll allow herself to think of what she's done from the perspective of a common human, one taught to consider all the unsavory realities of homicide. She's killed someone, a man who had a family, debts, a car. And she's taken his energy in the process. The rituals had guaranteed it. She places a hand over her pelvis, the spot near her belly button which flared with sensation as the man's life left his form and some of his vigor zipped into her. All her work for the masters of Aries culminated in taking the man's life. His death was the capstone, the bookend, the maraschino cherry. Necessary. The work incomplete without it.

Though she tries to feel sorrow, she possesses no remorse, no fear of retribution or punishment. Peach still understands killing indiscriminately is wrong. If she allows herself to think of killing other people—those not vetted and sanctioned for sacrifice—the emotions of regret and disgust bubble within. But not with the replay in her mind of Roman's demise: the tattoo gun shoved in his left ear canal, the hole she stomped in the center of his face. She intuits the man had his part to play in her story. He was the first human sacrificed to bring Perfect Peach to life. He'll always hold that distinction and Peach figures his death, aiding her in ways she has yet to ferret out, was the very pinnacle of his existence.

She looks at the shriveled flesh on her fingers in the dim light of the kitchen, the still of deep evening all around, and promises to make the tattooist a saint for the part he's played. Not a saint for the god of the Christians and Jews and Muslims, but for her. When it's all over, when her work is complete, she thinks she will decorate a wooden panel with his sacrosanct visage in rich dollops of vivid, oily paint. Sacramental robes exchanged for a high-buttoned plaid shirt, his hands lifted to preach her glory, tattoo gun in one fist, ink pot in the other. Roman Saucedo will be a transcendent idol. He will stand as an example for the others.

A bag sits on the table across from her. It's a beige plastic sack with a green alien logo printed on it. The creature's eyes are black almonds. She meets its gaze and knows it cannot see her, cannot see the special contents within the bag. Peach is too tired to do anything with it right now other than note it's something necessary to deal with. And deal with soon.

Another weak cry and she remembers the lamb still waits. She pushes herself up from the table and goes to the refrigerator. She heats up some of the unpasteurized goat milk she gives the lamb and closes her eyes, listens to the whir of the microwave plate spinning the liquid around and around with the occasional clunking sound as it catches on the revolving base. There's no need to test it on her wrist anymore. She has the heating down to a science. The scent of cream hits her nose.

The lamb continues his bleating and Peach goes to him, swinging her legs over the gates to enter the fenced off area of the living room. He rushes her thighs, bumps her with his soft forehead and rubs the lanolin from his skin onto her red dress. He pulls away and she can see his white wool smudged with a bit of blood. She looks down and can't see the red liquid on the crimson dress. She wonders how much of the tattooist's fluids she's managed to track into her car and her home. She'll have her work cut out for her with clean up. She recalls the last time she left flecks of red around her space, after the night she spray-painted deep ruby Vs onto major street intersections throughout Boise.

Peach attaches a nipple to the bottle and bends down to offer it to the lamb. He snatches at it with soft lips and rivulets of milk slip out of the corners of his mouth. She drops to her knees and holds the bottle while regarding the blotch of blood on the lamb's head. Both the animal and she have been marked by blood. She has the tattooist's blood mixed in the fresh ink on her scalp. She hadn't planned to massage his life force into her open pores but she'd been called to claim it and her tattoo as trophy. In the scant light, the blood on the lamb is merely a dark smear. It could be anything: soot, soil, oil. But Peach knows what it is.

It's power.

She pats the lamb on his back and closes her eyes again, the weariness taking over.

"I'm sorry I took your flock downtown," she says. The lamb slurps away. "I'm sorry your mother had to give birth to you in such foreign and stressful circumstances. You should have been born on grass, cold and yielding and green. I'm sorry for you, and for your mother and for your sister."

She calls to mind the work and planning it took to get the hundreds of sheep into downtown Boise. She remembers the warm slime on her arms plunged deep into the lambing ewe, pulling the second of two lives, a second lamb out of the sheep. She'd left the female with the mother and absconded with the male. She leaves the memory alone and comes back to the present, feels the glass container jerk against her palm as the baby takes his sustenance.

And Peach thinks nothing of her empathy for the lamb and her apparent inability to empathize over the spent life of the tattooist. Then she remembers the lamb still doesn't have a proper name. And then it comes to her.

He finishes the bottle of milk and she pulls the flexible nipple away from his mouth. She plants a kiss on his black nose, her lips coming away wet, the smell of animal and sour liquid permeating the back of her throat.

"Your name is Roman," she tells him and cups her fingers around his soft, warm ears. "You're named after a saint, a sacrifice, a helper of Perfect Peach."

02   RILEY

He must have slipped into sleep. Riley shoots up, the vertebrae in his spine cracking as they stack, and looks around the room for a clock. When his eyes locate one, digital numbers glowing in lime green, he sees it's just after 2am. The bedroom in which he finds himself is foreign. Heavy, dark drapes keep the room free from any light from outside and the headboard of the bed smells of cedar. An amber glow emanates from a night light shaped like the Sydney Opera House. He looks to his right and sees Nell Hyde, the stripper from Blaze Lounge he pursued and bedded, passed out next to him. Her form is splayed out at sharp, joint-bending angles and her sequined, black booty shorts are missing. Her neon green tube top is tucked under her large breasts and a sizable mole just above her right nipple rises and sinks with each inhalation and exhalation.

Riley immediately thinks of escape.

He's still drunk, but he's not so drunk to be experiencing brown outs—those stints of lost time and unrecorded awareness that aren't severe enough to be labeled as black outs. He recalls the sex he had with the stripper. Rather, the bouts of sex they'd had. Their rutting had been unusual, even compared to the backlog of Riley's varied and robust sexual experiences. She'd express moments of rapture, holding tight with her knees as she rode Riley. And then she would go slack, her limbs soft, and the spark of light in her eyes would dim. In this state, her body would automatically go through the motions of sex but he knew her mind was adrift in different seas. She'd murmur something about fire and the Australian town of Coober Pedy, train tracks and childhood monsters.

Though his hands are tingly, his vision slightly blurred, he's sober enough to realize something is wrong with the woman. And he has no desire to stick around and take the blame for her blitzed, drugged-out mind.

Riley rocks his hips around on the bed, testing to see if Nell will wake when he moves. Her body remains corpse-like and he stands in one fluid motion, pokes around the floor for his pants, stumbling only once and upon finding them, pulls them over his bare buttocks. He can't locate his shirt; his hands sweeping over the thick carpet and around the base of the bed produce nothing. There is a lamp on the bed stand but he won't risk clicking it on.

On a small armchair in the corner of the room lays a lump of something. Riley can't make it out so he goes over to it and feels at it. It's soft, knit. He holds it up close to his face, forgetful of what he wore to the strip club that night. The fabric is threadbare in some places and it smells of musky antiperspirant. He throws it back down.

The shirt belongs to Sev, the Australian poet with

control issues. Nell's boyfriend.

"Shit," he murmurs to himself. "I'm in the asshole's bedroom. If I'm here, where the hell is he?"

Logic and fear should partner in this moment, act to push him toward the exit of this unknown home and away from his dastardly doings. The thought of Sev returning, finding him leaving the jersey sheets and the embrace of his paramour should make him fly faster. But instead, Riley is torn. The reasonable part of Riley tells him to get out, go home and sleep off his drunk in his own king-sized bed. But the part of him that desires the wildness of life wins over.

Riley goes back to the bed and takes Nell by the shoulders and shakes her until she bats at him with limp hands. She keeps her eyelids closed and he leans over her with his face close enough for them to bump noses.

"You want to fuck again?" he asks and she answers with a nod, her head flopping around on her neck.

His callous, self-important screwing will need to be quick. Riley is hard from knowing he's in Sev's bedroom, having sex with the girlfriend Sev fought so hard to protect from Riley. The poet could open the bedroom door any moment and find himself a cuckold. This widens Riley's smile. Nell releases quick, quiet grunts while he works on her with his fingers, never opening her eyes to look at his face. He nearly enters her without a condom but then remembers to suit up before pushing in and spending millions of futures inside of her. He leaves her lying with her ear snuggling her shoulder, her ribcage cocked up and off the mattress. She looks to be in a strange sort of yoga pose: The Marionette du Riley or Congress of the Stripper.

"Get some sleep," he quips, but she doesn't respond. He can tell she's already passed out, from tiredness or chemicals or both. Her navel slowly sinks back down to the fitted sheet. On his way out of the bedroom, his whole foot—his good foot with all of his toes—catches on his lost shirt and he scoops it up and tucks it under his sweaty armpit. He sniffs and catches his own body odor and the funk of sex permeating the air in the room.

There is no desire to stay and poke around Sev's domain. He leaves the house, passing through as few rooms as possible to reach the exit. The night air is bracing; the flesh on his bare chest prickles and rises. Yet he doesn't put on the shirt. He feels raw and untouchable.

He looks back at the front door he's just shut behind him. It's a dusty brown color with a welcome mat at its base made of woven plaits of colorful fabric. He's happy he'll never see it again.

He tries to imagine Nell's face but it's already fading—her sharp A-line haircut, her fake tits. He's taken what he wanted from her. The pursuit of Nell had been undertaken to make Riley feel more manly and in control. The booze in his blood makes his memory of this night murky. But he knows he got her away from Sev and completed what he set out to do.

He won. He screwed. He now feels remarkable and accomplished.

There is a smile on his face as he walks to his car.

"Been there, fucked that," he says to the night.

DON'T WORRY.

PEACH & RILEY

ARE JUST GETTING STARTED.

THE BULL CHARGES

22 JUNE 15

THE BULL: CYCLE 2 OF *THE BLOOD ZODIAC*

AVAILABLE JUNE 2016

Pharmaceuticals
ARE GONE.
What do you do?

A dystopian, literary thriller set in an America without access to the drugs that keep us alive.

"This is without a doubt, the best dystopian book I have read this year."
- Top 500 Amazon Reviewer

CHEMICALS IS NOW AVAILABLE ON AMAZON AND OTHER ONLINE EBOOK RETAILERS.